The

The Archers' Castle is the second book in an exciting and action-packed saga about an Englishman who rose to becomes the captain of a company of English archers—and what he did that began changing medieval England in such a way that Britain would end up being an economic and military powerhouse that continues to punch far above its weight to this very day.

This book, like all the others in the series, was prepared many years ago for an unknown royal benefactor who wanted to know more about his real ancestors. The work itself was done by the monks of the Priory of St. Frideswide in Oxford, the monastery which Cardinal Wolsey dissolved and Henry the Eighth subsequently re-founded as Christ Church College after he broke with Rome. The many other books in this exciting medieval saga are also immediately available on Kindle and in print.

The initial book in the saga is *The Archer*. It is immediately available on Kindle and as a print book on Amazon. Readers may wish to read it first. The first book and the next five stories of the saga are available individually and in a collection of all six books entitled *The Archers Story*. There are subsequent collections and all of the stories are available individually as well.

Many of the parchments containing the exciting stories were found by Adrian Hogg some years ago in a trunk buried under a pile of rubble in the Bodleian Library basement. The stains on the parchments and the periodic slurring of the words suggests they were written by the unknown monks whilst they were visiting the taverns of medieval Oxford, notably the Bear and the King's Arms.

The assignment of the unknown monks was to translate and piece together what was left of numerous earlier biographies and records into one great history of Cornwall's Company of Archers and its relationship with the royal family. What was intended was something similar to the history the great Livy wrote for Rome so many years ago— with its emphasis on using the various participants' own words to describe what they were thinking and doing and seeing at the time.

Among the many problems the unknown monk and the subsequent authors of the Company's story said he had to overcome was that the exciting tales in some of the parchments contained so many surprises and often had missing parts where the mice had eaten them.

Another problem the monk noted, and perhaps the biggest, was that the parchments that had to be pieced together were written in various languages and different monks with different abilities translated them using their version of the English language and grammar. Some were written in Latin and Greek while others were in various versions of what is now called Middle English or Norman French. It was enough to drive a monk to drink or into comforting arms, and apparently it frequently did.

As a result of the great differences from one parchment record to the next, there are style and grammar differences and sometimes, particularly for the most important events, there are time overlaps when the monks used parchments from more than one source to present and describe certain of the more important events. Over-all, however, the exciting saga flows and reads rather well as it moves from one action packed event to the next in medieval England.

What follows in this particular volume was mostly taken from the parchments describing the adventures and battles of William, the commoner from Kent who rose in the years following King Richard's crusade to become the captain of what came to be known as Cornwall's Company of Archers. The particular events of William's life as the Commander of the Company were faithfully recorded by his lieutenant and scribe, Yoram of Damascus. Other sources were parchments from other scribes describing the activities and thoughts of William's priestly brother Thomas, his sons George and John, and several of his key lieutenants and sergeants.

The position of the Church and the royal family's hand-wringing senior servants has always been that the many changes and great excitement William and his archers caused in medieval England and the Holy Land were "God's Will." The monk initially in charge of pulling the various translations together into one great history of the company was obviously not so sure. According to him, the first person accounts and the descriptions and explanations of the people involved suggest that lusty men and modern weapons such as bladed pikes and longbows were a much more likely explanation.

There is no mistake about it—the books in the saga are a description of the dawn of Britain's rise to be a great military and merchant power and why so many members of the royal family have red hair.

Book Two

The Archers' Castle

Chapter One

We finally make it back to England.

People on the little Falmouth quay and the fishing
boats tied along it were standing up and looking as more
and more of our galleys came into Falmouth harbour. It was
no wonder that they were—Harold's galley was in front and
he was leading a long string of our galleys towards the
entrance of the River Fal. And right behind them was one of
our cogs under its captain sergeant, Martin, the archer from
Yorkshire. If my older brother Thomas's count is correct,
almost all of our boats have arrived.

Of our twenty-one galleys and two single-masted cargo
cogs which sailed from Malta, all but one of our galleys were
now in Falmouth's harbour. The missing galley somehow
disappeared along the way just as did two of the prizes we
had taken out of Tunis.

We are a strong force even without our missing galleys;
that is for sure. As of today we have twenty galleys and two
cargo cogs here in Falmouth harbour with eleven hundred
and eighty-eight men including ten of the original one

hundred and ninety-two archers who set out from Windsor seven years ago to go crusading with King Richard.

Our men include more than three hundred rowers we hired in the ports we visited to help row our prizes. They will be paid and returned to their home ports in Lisbon and along the way when we return to our home base in Cyprus.

Those are the numbers if none of our men have run since we last counted them. What they mean is that we have arrived in England with a big problem—we are seriously short of men. That is because all of our galleys are big and modern sea-going two-deckers with at least thirty oars on each side. They are all big and modern because we burned the prizes we took that only had one rowing deck and all the bigger ones that were not immediately seaworthy.

Most sea-going war galleys need a crew of at least one hundred men to help row them and set their sails and lay their courses. It means that we will have to recruit a large number of new fighting men to join us if we are to return to the Holy Land with all our galleys. And that is likely to be impossible since experienced fighting men are hard to find because they are inevitably the vassals of some lord. As a result, we will almost certainly be forced to leave some of our galleys behind when we return to the Holy Land to earn more coins by carrying cargos between the various ports and refugees to safety.

My brother Thomas thinks we should immediately being recruiting new men from amongst the village slaves and serfs and the second sons of the franklins and teach them to push arrows out of a longbow and fight. I fear he is right about that just as he is usually right about everything else. If he is, it means we will likely have to leave some of our galleys behind because we cannot adequately crew them with enough fighting men to do the rowing.

Leaving some of the galleys we took as prizes behind when we return to the Holy Land to earn more coins is almost certain. That is because we long ago decided to use only fighting men to do our rowing instead of slaves as is the custom of the Moors and Venetians.

What Thomas and I learned from our experiences is that having more fighting men on each of our galleys inevitably gave us a great advantage when it comes to fighting off the Moorish pirates when they come after the cargos and refugees we are carrying in their search for slaves and ransoms. *There is nothing better than outnumbering your enemies when you have to fight them; it is in the Bible according to Thomas.*

Something else we will be doing whilst in England is trying to learn more about an interesting cargo we have captured. The cog Albert and his crew cut out when we raided the harbour at Tunis is full of little wooden chests containing balls and bricks of some kind of smelly flower paste.

My priestly brother Thomas thinks the paste is the same apothecary's compound the poxed captain was being fed when we bought our first boats off him—the two galleys and the cog we bought with the coins we found in the chests we took from the Bishop of Damascus after Thomas killed the murdering bastard.

It probably is the same paste because he is usually right, my brother Thomas is, because he knows so much—being as he memorized some of the Bible and read all nine of the books in the monastery and some of the scrolls before he walked away and left it to rescue me from being a serf pulling a plough and his arse from the clutches of a lecherous abbot. He did so by taking me crusading with the untrustworthy Norman who is now our king even though he is being held for ransom somewhere.

The paste is very interesting. It takes the pain away from wounds. At least it did for poor Peter when he got his hand sliced and it rotted so bad he died despite the barber bleeding him quite prodigiously. Worth its weight in gold to people with broken bones and wounded soldiers and sailors is what it is.

I wonder where the paste comes from. Thomas thinks we should ask the Saracens where they are getting it the next time we catch one. He thinks we could earn a lot of gold bezant coins selling it, coins we will surely need if we are to carry out our plan to advance my son.

Chapter Two

Carrying the sad news.

"We spent much too much time trying to get what was left of the archers back to England and dreaming about all the big things we would do for little George when we finally got him here."

"Aye, and not enough time thinking of practical things—like where we will spend the winter and how we will find food and warm clothes for him and our men."

My brother Thomas and I were standing on the bank of the River Fal. Those were my priestly brother's comments and my reaction to the activity we were watching on the river and the shouting and cursing we could hear coming from the galleys and cogs out on the river.

Our boats were trying to make their way upstream against the river's current. And kindest thing that can be said about the situation is that things were not going very well at the moment.

"They will come up further if we unload them." Thomas mused.

"Aye, but not by much, goddamnit," was my frustrated response.

"Maybe we are trying to find a place to camp on the wrong river," Thomas suggested. "There are other rivers in England you know."

Thomas was right, of course. But we are here for a good reason and we are doing the best we can. At the moment we were using a couple of our galleys in an effort to pull our two heavily loaded cogs up the River Fal from the estuary at its mouth.

What we were trying to do was get them as far up the river as they can go before they touch bottom and can go no further—which was turning out to be not very far at all.

The galleys themselves, of course, can be rowed further upstream than the cogs because they have flatter bottoms and are not held down into the water by the weight of the high masts and the heavy cargos each of the cogs were carrying. The heavy cargos, of course, being the weapons and Saracen iron we took from Acre and the amphorae of grain and oil they are carrying.

The cargos our galleys and cogs were carrying were important. We needed the weapons to defend ourselves and the grain to make the bread and brew the ale we drink to break our fast when the sun arrives each morning on its daily trip around the world.

My brother Thomas and I were standing not far from the edge of the river on the side of a gentle hill that runs down to the river. From here we could see and hear the activity on the cogs and the galleys pulling them.

Our sailing sergeant, Harold the former master of a London cog and a galley slave that we had bought and freed when we bought our first boats from their poxed owner, was obviously chivvying them along and dissatisfied with the results. Every so often we could hear his curses and orders all the way up here on the riverbank.

"Harold is in fine form today, Thomas said. I just nodded and continued to look and listen.

Looking down the river past our boats we could see the roofs of the hovels in the little fishing village of Falmouth. They are off there in the distance at the mouth of the river where the harbour begins. It is harvest time and ever since we got here the local serfs and churls have been working in the fields around us from dawn to dusk—not that they will get much for all their efforts. According to Thomas, the land is so poor that even the Romans did not bother to build a road to Cornwall.

And it is hard work the serfs are doing as I damn well know; I used to be one of them before me Mum died and Thomas came back from the monastery to learn me to scribe and sum and take me away to go crusading with the King.

We are here because we are trying to kill two birds with one arrow—get to Lord Edmund's wife so we can tell her he is dead by the Saracens, and find a place where we can establish a winter camp and protect our boats and coins whilst we recruit and train more archers. We need more men who know how to use a longbow and are trained to fight at sea so we can take our galleys back out to the Holy Land and earn coins by taking Moorish boats as prizes and carrying refugees and cargos and such from port to port.

"Well Captain," Thomas inquired with a smile and a twinkle in his eye, "what are you going to do now?"

"I do not know. But look sharp, my dear priestly brother. Here comes trouble."

Riding towards us were a couple of horsemen. We stood quietly and watched as they rode up. Neither looked very threatening though one was clearly a knight and wearing a shirt of chain mail armour similar to the one I always wear under my long baggy-sleeved tunic and Thomas always wears under his hooded priest's cassock.

Neither of the riders was wearing a helmet nor carrying a drawn sword so we did not draw our swords or string the bows we always carry slung over our shoulders.

The knight was an older white haired man with a genial smile and a big bushy beard. He held up his hand in a friendly greeting as he approached.

"Hello Hello," the knight said with a distinctly Norman accent as he swung himself off his horse and dismounted with his hand held out and a friendly smile on his face.

"I am Percy. Sir Percy actually. The Earl of Cornwall's sheriff for Falmouth. I have a knight's fee and a hovel on the other side of the village."

"Hello, Sir Percy," I said as I took his hand and smiled back and named myself.

"I am William, captain of what is left of King Richard's Company of Archers and those galleys out there in the river are some of the prizes we took whilst returning to England. We are trying to get them up the river to someplace where we can camp for the winter. Hopefully we can find a place before the leaves begin to fall." *I did not mention that I had bought a title on Cyprus—it would not mean much to an Englishman, or to anyone else for that matter. But every little bit helps as it says in the Bible.*

"And this is my brother, Thomas. He is the Bishop of the Bekka Valley and the Company's priest in addition to being an archer. We were not aware the Earl had a sheriff here in Falmouth or we would have come to visit you and announced ourselves."

It still feels funny to name Thomas a bishop and me as a Cyprus lord—but the titles were cheap and we bought them fair and square. We did so with our prize money because we thought they might be helpful when dealing with those who still respect the Church and those who favour the nobility because they have useless daughters they need to marry off.

"Oh, no bother. No bother at all. I am new here myself. Indeed, me and my wife do not even have a proper place for you to know about—just an old hovel out beyond the town is all."

Ten minutes of friendly conversation and it was obvious Sir Percy was a harmless old soul who was grateful for the excitement of our arrival and anxious to hear stories about our adventures crusading with King Richard in the Holy Land.

Percy's man Otto I was not too sure about. He looked us over carefully and listened intently while I gave a very general description of where we have been and a fairly lame explanation of why we are here.

"Our archers are from all over England so we probably should have continued on to London, it being in the middle of things so to speak. But Falmouth is the closest port to Lord Edmund's fief at Trematon and we promised him we would look after his wife if he fell."

Sir Percy beamed his approval.

"It is good men you are for keeping your word to Lord Edmund. His widow and children will appreciate it, poor things. I did not know him, of course, since I am newly arrived but everything I have heard about him has been good.

Then we talked about many things in an effort to get to know one another—Falmouth and the local community,

Percy's years of war in France, and our plans to stay over the winter and what we might do to recruit men to take back to the Holy Land with us to help us rescue more refugees. Sir Percy smiled and nodded his head enthusiastically when I said we hoped to go back to rescue more people from the Saracens in the spring.

What we did not tell the old fellow was the real reason we are intent on going back to the Holy Land to rescue people—to earn more of their coins and jewels. *What we have learnt is people with coins are willing to pay them to us to carry them to safety when they think the Saracens will kill them or take them as slaves if they do not escape. Similarly willing to pay us are the merchants and pilgrims who want their cargos and themselves to travel in war galleys the Moorish pirates are not likely to attack.*

We were also very carefully not to mention anything to our amiable visitor about our plans for young George or our intention to establish a permanent base of some kind in Cornwall—and no one, not even Sir Percy, in any way even hinted as to whether he supported Richard or John in the argument which seems to be raging as to whether or not John should remain on the throne if Richard is still alive or be his heir if he is not.

All Sir Percy and his man know when they finally rode away to friendly smiles and waves is that we are what is left of a crusading company of English archers and a bishop forced from his flock by the Saracens—and we intend to stay here for a while before we return to the Holy Land to carry more refugees and pilgrims to safety.

What they also did not learn was anything about our humble origins or the questionable titles we bought in Cyprus or our plans for my son George. They do not even know Thomas is my brother—which is a secret we have decided to keep until we get a better lay of the land and know how the local Earl will react to our being here.

But at least the sheriff knows enough to speak the bastardized Norman dialect of Somerset and Kent that is used by the crusaders and people are starting to call English. The people in Falmouth village and hereabouts speak a local dialect we can hardly understand.

"Ah well. Back to the business at hand," Thomas sighed.

"What about pulling the galleys out of the water over there between the trees? The ground looks solid and it is level enough with a bit of a slope so the rain and piss waters will run off. We could put the men's tents and hovels over there by the trees."

"Aye, you could be right, Thomas, you could be right."...

******

"Samuel, the sun has just come up, the wind is from the east out of the sun, and you are rowing and tacking into the wind. You have only thirty experienced Marine archers and ten sailors on board your galley because you are out with a skeleton crew so you can pack in as many refugees as possible. Your lookout on the mast has just reported seeing two Tunisian war galleys dead ahead of you. They are turning towards you and have the wind. What orders do you give?"

Harold is the master sergeant of our sailors and that was the kind of question he and Thomas and I had been asking all of our sergeant captains for the past three days—prior to selecting sergeants to captain the six galleys we had decided to send back to Cyprus to carry refugees and other coin-paying passengers and cargos to the Holy Land and other destinations.

What we were doing was talking with all our prize captains at the same time about what the captain of a Company galley should do when various events happen. Doing so was something Thomas suggested. He said such "make believe talk" was quite helpful for him when he was at the monastery being taught how to behave like a priest.

"There is a lot more to acting like a priest than just mumbling prayers in Latin so the common folk need someone to explain what God wants them to do."

I did not think much of the idea, but I went along with it because Thomas is so well educated, what with memorizing some of the Bible and reading all nine books at the monastery. Thomas did it, got his education I mean, before he left the monastery to rescue me from being a plough boy and take me crusading with King Richard's very own Company of Archers—the Company I now have the honour to command.

After listening Thomas for a while, I could most honestly say the "make believe talking" for our galley captains has been interesting and helpful, at least for me. Hopefully it has been for them as well.

What we have been doing for the past three days is confronting all of our sergeant captains with different situations and asking what orders they would give and what they would expect their men and their galley to do after they give them.

Their first answers, as you might imagine, range from quite the right thing to do under the circumstances to damn foolish, particularly from those who are new sergeant captains as a result of successfully taking a prize out of Tunis and sergeanting it to Cornwall. Then everyone talked about their answers until they all understand the best orders to give under the circumstances and why they should be given. *At least we hope they all understand what they should do and say—and remember to act when the time comes.*

When we finished talking with the sergeant captains and listening to their answers Thomas and Harold and I selected the sergeants whose galleys are to sail back to Cyprus and the Holy Land before the storm season arrives. *And then began wondering how many of the galleys and which of our men we would never see again.*

******

In a couple of days six of our galleys will begin sailing and rowing their way back to Cyprus and the Holy Land along the same basic route we followed to get here a couple of weeks ago.

Not all of the galleys and cogs we brought to England a few days ago are going back. One of the galleys had already left for London with three of the surviving original archers who wanted to go home, a dozen or so of the English galley slaves we freed, and miscellaneous sailors and soldiers and refugees. They are mostly men who originally came from London or thereabouts and want to try to walk to their old homes from there.

After the men are dropped off the galley's sergeant captain will try to buy some sacks of grain we can grind for flour and use to brew our ale. He will use the coins we gave him to buy them at the big market for merchants selling grain near London's long quay.

We know he can find them there because I myself helped carry sacks of grain from that very market to the cog that carried us to Cyprus when I was a young lad and our company of archers went crusading with King Richard.

There were one hundred and ninety two of us then; now we are only ten here in England and another seven still in the east for one reason or another. Mostly they are with Yoram on Cyprus.

Another galley and both of our cogs will soon be following the London galley and go east and west to make many more stops at the smaller ports along both coasts. They will be going all the way to Newcastle and Blackpool with stops in the smaller ports along the way to land recruiting parties and buy supplies in addition to dropping off a couple of returning archers and various others.

Before our galleys and cogs can sail from here, however, we will have to unload the coin chests they are carrying—and that means finding a place where we can safely store their cargos and pull some of our galleys out of the water

Those galleys we pull out of the water will be laid up for the winter because we do not have enough men to crew them—both because of desertions as we returned from the Holy Land and because of our intention to honour our promise to discharge the men who want to go home. Compounding the problem is that almost five hundred of our best fighting men will be staying with us to guard our boats and coins and other valuables.

Also staying with us in Cornwall will the two hundred or so likely looking recruits we picked up along the way and have begun training as apprentice archers.

It is a long process to train archers to use a longbow. They need to develop strong arms and learn how to use their bows and care for them. And our archers need even more training than most because we would be using them on both land and sea.

Surprisingly enough, at least to me, most of the hundreds of galley slaves we acquired and freed when we cut the galleys out of Tunis, including more than half the Englishmen, have volunteered to stay on with us as sailors and make the return trip to Cyprus and the Holy Land.

Some probably to get closer to home before they run; but many, it seems, do not have anywhere to go and do not know what else to do. Poor sods.

Most of the former slaves who are still with us are lost souls who do not have any idea what to do with themselves. A couple of dozen made their marks to train as archer apprentices and others are still with us because they are going to travel towards their homes on the Company galleys and cogs we will be sending to Newcastle and Blackpool with stops along the way.

We expect many of the archers and slaves will come back. People die in the villages and things change so it is hard to go home after being away for years.

Thomas and I are good examples of why it is hard to go home; there is now nothing in the village to attract us and we would be damned and dead before we would return to being serfs for whoever is the local lord these days.

******

Most of our galleys heading for Cyprus and the Holy Land in the next few days will be gone until about this time next year, if not longer. And that is if they are lucky and do not get taken by the Moors or go down in a storm along the way.

And yes, damn it, I made a mistake; we should have sent most or all of the prize galleys back to Cyprus as soon as we took them off the Moors and got them to Malta.

In any event, if things go as we hope, over the winter we would be training up more longbow archers and recruiting experienced pilots and sailor sergeants here in England. If we were successful we would be able to send the rest of our galleys out to the Holy Land next year with full crews.

It is experienced sea pilots and longbow archers we need most of all and, after them, strong young men we can train to be archers—particularly Englishmen and Welshmen since we need men we can trust.

Sailors and men who know how to use a sword are not such a big a problem. If necessary we can recruit them along the way as we have done in the past.

Accordingly, the galleys and cogs going to Newcastle and Blackpool will put recruiting parties ashore at various ports along the way and then pick them and their recruits up on the way back. At least that was the current plan.

There is a lot of shipping and sailor men on the Thames below London so all of our boats going north past the Thames will call in there for a visit and try to recruit in London and the various ports and quays and wharves serving it.

In addition to sailors who are also pilots and who have made multiple visits to the Holy Land and have extensive experience as the sergeants of sailors, our recruiting parties are particularly looking for experienced longbow men and likely young men we can apprentice to be archers, but only if they are willing to make to make their marks on our company's roll to serve in the east aboard our galleys and cogs.

Also, at Thomas' request, our recruiting sergeants have been told to keep an eye out and pass the word to let the priests and merchants know we are looking for lively young boys who might be smart enough to be learned to scribe and do sums and such. Thomas wants them for the school he intends to establish for my son to attend so George can be learned to talk the Latin and scribe and sum.

The sergeant captains of the cogs and the galleys being used for recruiting and supply purposes and the sergeants in charge of the recruiting parties do not know it yet, of course, but they are being tested.

Each will be given a goodly sum of silver coins he can use to buy the tents and clothes we need and to hire fishing boats and passages for any additional recruits and supplies if the boat he is sergeanting is not large enough to carry everything.

They will also each be taking one of the paste chests to show to the merchants they meet. We want to know what value the paste might have and who might buy it—and who among our sergeants is capable of dealing with merchants.

Hopefully the galleys' sergeant captains and the recruiting sergeants will use the coins well and get results. If they do we can promote them; if not, at least we will know that they are not up to bigger things.

Our biggest need of all, however, was not likely to be filled—for dependable fighting men who can also scribe and do sums, and thus are capable of being sergeants captaining major outposts such as Yoram and Randolph are captaining for us in Cyprus and Alexandria.

The chance of recruiting such men was slim to none. Thomas is probably right when he says we would have to find likely young boys and train them from scratch if we are to continue to grow a powerful company for George to take over when we are too old to sail and fight.

Anyhow, growing our own sergeants is what Thomas wants to do so that was why we were looking for likely young lads who can be learned and brought along with young George. Thomas thinks he has already found two such boys in Falmouth.

What we were hoping was in the years before George and Thomas's students are ready to take over we would be able to use sergeants who can be joined with scriveners who know how to read and do sums. In the meantime, we have decided to send some of the prize galleys with little more than skeleton crews back to Cyprus for Yoram to send on to the Holy Land ports—and keep six hundred or so of our current strength in Cornwall.

Well, it is six hundred if we include the hundred and forty or so men who will be sailing in our cogs and recruiting galleys and the two hundred or so apprentice archers we recruited from the nearby villages and are now training.

******

Every one of the galleys heading to Cyprus and on to the Holy Land is a prize galley we took out of Tunis; and every sergeant captaining it except one is the original sergeant of its prize crew.

Each of them will sail with the smallest possible crew of sailors and fighting men so their galley can sail between

Cyprus and the Holy Land ports with as many refugees and their coins as its sergeant captain can squeeze in.

Except for the one man Harold removed for gross incompetence, the captains will be the prize captains who got their galleys to England. They were all given the opportunity to keep their commands and they all chose to do so—and in virtually every case were astonished to find themselves elevated above the status in which they had expected to spend their entire lives. *Thomas and I certainly know the feeling.*

The sergeants who became prize captains and their sergeants and crews were selected before we visited Tunis from the men already serving with us. *They got their prizes all the way to England so we are giving them a chance to keep them.*

Where we have made some changes are in the galleys' pilots and in the sergeants of their sailors and fighting men.

There seem to be some good sailor men, including a number of boat owners and boat masters among the slaves we freed when we took the heathen galleys. Some of the best of them will soon be on their way to Cyprus and the Holy Land; others we are keeping with us in Cornwall to crew the galleys which we will be temporarily pulling ashore.

Each of our six sergeants heading for the Holy Land as the sergeant captain of a galley is authorized to maintain his crew by signing up replacement archers and other fighting men if they need additional rowers. They are also authorized to sign-up sailors and short-term rowers in the ports they visit along the way.

They are not, however, to recruit more men than they need for replacements except for experienced archers, and particularly longbow men who are to be recruited whenever they can be found no matter where they come from.

It was explained over and over again in the "make believe talking" meetings why the galley captains are to keep their crews as small as possible and still be able to fight off pirates—so as to allow for the largest possible numbers of coin paying refugees, pilgrims, and merchants.

The "make believe talking" is Thomas' idea and it absolutely amazes the men; they, like me, had never heard of such a thing. But they took to it with surprising enthusiasm and all of them claim to have learned a lot. I certainly did whilst I was helping Harold and Thomas learn them what to do under various circumstances.

A big part of our problem will be to keep the sergeants honest when there are so many coins involved. That is why all the passengers the galleys pick up in the Holy Land ports will be delivered to Cyprus and interviewed by Yoram on the Cyprus quay as soon as they arrive.

As you might imagine, the big question every passenger will be asked privately as soon as he steps on the quay is how much he actually paid for his passage. And it better be what each of our sergeant captains turns over to Yoram—the passengers will be interviewed and checked off when they arrive and corrupt sergeant captains and any of their sergeants and crew men involved will be immediately killed or discharged.

At least, that is what we told the sergeant captains and their sergeants and that is what appears in the instruction parchments the galleys are carrying to Yoram and Randolph. The sergeants had better believe it—for Randolph and Yoram have indeed been ordered to immediately kill anyone who holds out on us.

****** Bishop Thomas

I rode out of camp wearing the gown and mitre I took off the bishop I killed in Latika. I am off to find Lord Edmund's widow and give her the sad news of Edmund's death—although I am certainly not going to tell her it was a soldier's mercy from William because Edmund was so grievously wounded and pained. William is going to stay behind in Falmouth with Harold and George.

While I am gone William and Harold will organize our men for the winter since it looks like we will be staying right here in Cornwall—and that means training them for land warfare using horse bowmen in the Saracen style and the new bladed pikes our smiths made for us before we left

Cyprus. And, all the while, he will be trying to recruit new men from the surrounding villages.

William and Harold are also going to begin a week or more of training and role playing for the captains of our cogs and galleys and their sergeants. Harold has more than proved his worth. He is still the sergeant captain of our best galley but he is also now the master sergeant in charge of all of our galleys and cogs in British waters.

******

About a dozen of our steadiest archers and soldiers travelled with me to visit Edmund's wife at his fief in Trematon. Three of the four horses we were able to buy in Falmouth carried our tents and supplies. I rode the fourth because rank has its privileges as it says somewhere in the Bible. They were all farm horses but better than having none.

I was in no hurry and the men were walking—so we made slow time. It took three days on a rough and meandering cart path before Edmund's isolated little castle came into view. It only rained one day and after all those weeks at sea it was rather relaxing to walk along the rough track and watch the local serfs labouring to bring in the harvest.

Seeing the men and women working in the fields brought back memories of being a serf myself and they were not good; I was pleased to be looking at the serfs work instead of being one of them; most of my men, I suspect, felt the same way.

No one bothered us or asked for a toll and we certainly drew a number of curious looks and friendly waves from the men and women working in the fields. Not having lords and their knights periodically ask for tolls to cross their lands is one of Cornwall's great benefits. Unfortunately it comes about because there are so few of them—the land is apparently so poor its revenues cannot support them.

We bought all the available horses and carts and wagons we could find in Falmouth and in the smaller villages around it. So now we have a grand total of four horses and three wagons. Hopefully we will so be able to buy some more. The Falmouth merchants all said there will be more horses available when the harvest is in and the monthly fair comes to town in a couple of weeks.

I certainly hope so. The four horses we have acquired so far were not very useful for riding. Plough horses rarely are. *And the lack of horses, of course, put paid to William's idea of forming a cavalry of horse archers of the type we watched the Saracens use against us; having our own cavalry will have to wait until we can find more horses and some of the archers can be learned to ride.*

******

My first impression as Trematon Castle came into view was not particularly encouraging. Both its keep and the courtyard inside its curtain wall were rather small. It did not even have a moat or gate tower, just a drawbridge over a small mud pond in front of the gate, and no outer bailey, not even a dirt ring fence to keep in the livestock. Even more worrisome, its curtain wall was not very high. *I wonder why it is so low?*

The nearby village where the castle's serfs and churls live looked to be as poor as the castle—no more than five or six wooden hovels and what looked to be a long-deserted little church. Not one of the hovels had a chimney. It is all very much like the little village where William and I lived until the Abbot took a look at my arse and carried me off to learn to pray and please him.

Our new acquired fortified farm house on Cyprus near the Limassol city walls looks to already be as strong or stronger than Trematon despite having neither a moat nor a drawbridge—and Yoram, our sergeant captaining our shipping post on Cyprus, is desperately working to strengthen it.

******

Our approach to the castle caused some anxiety and the drawbridge over the small pond in front of the gate began to be hauled up as we slowly walked up the path towards its gate.

I ordered the men to move back and led my horse slowly forward by myself while I waved my cross at the faces that began appearing at the arrow slits on wall.

"Who are you and what do you want?" came the hail.

"I am the Bishop of the Bekka Valley with news from the Holy Land about Lord Edmund."

A few minutes later the drawbridge creaked noisily as it was slowly lowered—and then dropped back to the ground with a crash and a splash from the mud puddle it landed in.

A few seconds later the old wooden gate in the castle's curtain wall opened and an elderly man came out wearing an old fashioned Saxon helmet and carrying a spear. He watched impassively as I slowly led my horse over the bridge and into the enclosure beyond the curtain wall. My men stayed on the cart path and did not attempt to follow me.

The drawbridge over the pond slowly rose behind me and the gate closed with a slam as soon as I entered the courtyard. Then there was a loud banging sound as the spear carrying guard and another man dropped a big wooden cross bar into place to seal the gate.

In the background I could hear the creaking as someone slowly cranked the drawbridge back up.

An anxious looking woman with a strong chin and her hair tied up in a knot came out of the low and narrow entrance door into the castle's keep with a couple of young girls clinging to her arms. She watched impassively as I dismounted and handed the reins of my horse to a rheumy eyed old man who walked up and held his hand out for them without saying a word.

******

The look on my face was all the woman needed to see— she burst into tears and clutched the girls to her.

"He is dead?"

"Aye, God rest his soul, he is. I am truly sorry to have to tell you that Lord Edmund is dead. A big rock was catapulted over the wall and hit him in the head. He never felt a thing."

Actually that was a lie. Edmund took a Saracen arrow in the shoulder and the rot set in. It took two weeks for him to die and at the end William did the right thing and gave him a soldier's mercy on the night he led what was left of our company over the south wall and we ran for it.

I watched without saying a word as the girls began sobbing and clinging to their mother while she tried to pull herself together and console them. The children must have been very young when Edmund left his family to go crusading. No wonder he was so concerned about them when he knew he was dying.

Finally the Edmund's wife turned her attention back to me.

With her arms still around the weeping girls, she used a nod of her head and a sad smile to motion me to enter. Six or seven men and women stood about in the yard and watched with increasingly sad faces as I ducked my head and entered. They instinctively understood the sorrowful news I was bearing.

******

"I have feared this day ever since the damn fool left," she told me as we walked into the castle's little great hall.

"He had to go, you know. The new Earl in Restormel Castle passed on the entire scutage the king levied on Cornwall and demanded Edmund either pay it or join Richard on his crusade so the Earl's brother would not have to go. And, of course, since we have no revenues, he could not pay it; so off he went with Richard."

I gave her twenty gold bezant coins the next morning after I conducted a prayer service for Edmund in the little village church. I lied with a great deal of sincerity in my voice and told her Lord Edmund entrusted the bezants to me to give to her in the event he fell.

I think she knew I was telling a lie but she thanked me profusely—and told me the bezants would be greatly appreciated because they would enable her and her children continue to live in the castle.

"After they are gone," she said that evening with a great sigh after the girls had gone off to the bed they shared, "I do not know what we will do."

I stayed for five days and we talked and talked and talked. Edmund's lady, her name is Dorothy and she was the daughter of a minor knight with a small knight's fee manor in Derbyshire, wanted to know everything about Edmund's life and the Holy Land—and the fate of the three local men who had accompanied him and the archers who joined him.

It was quite a tale, and often sad; and it took some time to tell.

******

Lady Dorothy and I were in the castle's little "great hall" just finishing a meal of bread and onion soup on the fifth day of my visit when one of her serfs came rushing in to report a group of men approaching on horseback.

I do not know why, perhaps I had a premonition, but I went to the keep's door and told the archers who were waiting for me in the castle bailey to go into to the stables and stay out of sight.

"But arm yourselves and be ready to fight if I call or it sounds like trouble."

Then I went back into the keep and re-seated myself at the long wooden table. The table and the stone staircase up to the castle's sleeping room almost filled the castle's very small great hall.

Someone in our camp must have spread news of Edmund's death for it was the Earl's youngest brother with four of his men who entered the hall. They entered as I was finishing my soup. His name as he named himself in Norman French was Ralph, Sir Ralph, and he was a smelly bearded fellow with no apparent sympathy or concern for Lady Dorothy.

He was not very respectful of priests and bishops either.

"I see you already know about your husband," he sneered at Lady Dorothy when he saw me sitting at the table slurping up my soup.

"Well that makes it easier. I came to tell you about your husband's death and help you move out."

"Move? Why should I move? This is Edmund's home and my children and I are Edmund's heirs. The King and the Church were quite clear that the families of anyone who fell would not lose their places."

"You will move because Lord Baldwin, the Earl of Cornwall, wants you to move. You have not paid your share of the King's taxes for two years and now Lord Baldwin needs to collect them more than ever. In case you have not heard, King Richard is captured and a ransom has to be raised, a big ransom."

Richard is alive? I will be damned.

"Now go up the stairs and get your things together. And do not take anything belonging to Edmund. We are keeping it to apply against your taxes."

And with that he grabbed her by the arm and thrust her towards the stone stairs that led to the living space above the hall.

The serf who had brought us the news about the riders and greeted them at the gate had come in behind Sir Ralph and his men. I did not know his name but he was standing against the wall listening to the conversation when I motioned him over and whispered an order into his ear:

"Go out back to the stables and tell my men to come around and wait by the door to the keep—and to be ready to charge in if there is a fight."

Then I injected myself into the conversation.

"I am sorry Sir Knight, but King Richard's law is quite clear. Widows of loyal nobles who fall on a crusade are to retain their lands and keeps without the payment of taxes for their lifetimes and those of their children."

It is all ox shite, of course. I am making it up.

"What is that you say? And who the hell are you?"

"I am Thomas, Bishop of Bekka and Lady Dorothy's confessor. And until he left the Holy Land I had the honour to be the confessor of our dear King Richard."

More ox shite. I never talked to the murdering bastard.

"I do not care who you are, she is leaving."

And with that he took Lady Dorothy by the arm and started to pull her towards the stone stairs leading to the room above the hall.

"I would not do that if I were you," I say with a snarl not at all appropriate for a man of the cloth.

"At least not until I give you your last rites. If you touch Lady Dorothy again you and your men will surely never leave this place alive. Best you open the door and take a look out into the bailey before you do something really stupid and get yourself killed."

It was one of Sir Ralph's men who opened the great hall's door at knight's nodded order—and jumped back in fright.

Seeing half a dozen swords and iron tipped arrows pointed at your chest will do that for you every time. Particularly when the men holding them look like the ferocious villains they are—which is how most escaped galley slaves and soldiers newly home from the crusades tend to look.

"Who are those men? What is going on here?" Sir Ralph demanded angrily as he turned and looked at me.

"They are some of Lord Edmund's retainers newly returned from fighting in the crusades."

That was a lie too. But why not—in for a copper, in for a gold.

******

As soon as the Earl's brother departed mumbling his threats I sent one of my men on a horse to carry a message to William describing the situation. I told him I intended to stay at the castle for a while longer in case Sir Ralph returns.

I also suggested William change the nature of our men's training to emphasize fighting on land and be prepared to march on Trematon on a moment's notice. I would, I informed my brother, send messengers if we need assistance.

And then, as a precaution and without telling Lady Dorothy, I sent three of my men and all three of my remaining horses to the little hill that rises about two miles away and overlooks the castle. They were to camp there as our lookouts and stay out of sight. We would send food and water out to them

If any armed men appear one of my lookouts is to ride to the castle and warn us; the other two are to immediately ride back to our camp by the river and inform William as to the size and strength of the new arrivals. I also made sure the castle's water barrel and little cistern were filled and quietly assigned fighting positions to my remaining men.

I did not mention my precautions to Edmund's poor lady. She was already distraught enough as it is.

It is a good thing I prepared. Three days later Sir Ralph returned with a number of armed men and his brother, Lord Baldwin, the Earl of Cornwall. They had ridden over from the Earl's seat at Restormel Castle.

Hmm. It is harvest time and they brought almost half a hundred men from Restormel who should be working in the fields. Trematon must be more important than it looks. Or maybe Lord Baldwin is particularly stupid or does not care if his people do not have enough to eat this winter.

This time they did not get in so easily. Not until his men pulled far enough back at my insistence did we lower the drawbridge over the pond, and then only long enough for Sir Ralph and the Earl to cross over and reach the gate in the castle's curtain wall.

I opened the gate a crack and spoke with them with half a dozen or so of my guards behind me in case they tried to push their way in. The rest were up on the walls keeping watch with their bows strung and their arrows ready to be snatched up and launched.

Their message surprised me and I told them as much.

Sir Ralph, it seems, is now offering to marry Edmund's widow. Her marriage, of course, would extinguish any rights she might have to the castle and make Sir Ralph the undisputed owner of both the castle and Lady Dorothy.

I raised my eyebrows, waved my cross to bless them, and agreed to convey the offer to her and get back to them.

"Tell her to hurry up and make up her mind," Baldwin demanded rather arrogantly.

"Until she accepts my brother no one gets in or out."

His Norman lordship was quite full of himself and seemed to think he held the upper hand—which, in a sense, he did.

Baldwin is a rat faced little bastard and my initial impression was he is even more arrogant and stupid than his brother. Taking his men away from the harvest proves it.

"I will take what you have said as a threat to do violence and I am sure Lady Dorothy and her men will too," I responded rather harshly.

"So be warned yourself. Until Lady Dorothy decides to remarry and chooses your brother, you and your men would be well advised to stay far away from Trematon's walls— because in a couple of minutes I am going to tell her guards it is time for them to begin breaking your blockade even if it means doing injuries to you both."

Actually, I made a mistake; we should have killed them both right then and there while the drawbridge was up behind them and they could not get away. Ah well, done is done. I have made many mistakes in my life have I not?

After handing out a few more irate threats and warnings the two nobles hurried away and the wall in the curtain gate slammed shut behind them. Only then did the drawbridge begin to go down so they could cross the pond and return to their waiting men.

Their heads were together and they were whispering and waving their hands and looking back at the castle as they crossed the bridge. My response on behalf of Lady Dorothy was obviously not the cowering agreement they expected.

Within minutes the drawbridge was back up and we watched from the walls as the Earl's men spread out and surrounded Trematon. That is when I climbed to castle turret and waved a piece of linen to signal one of my lookouts on the hill to gallop for Falmouth to fetch William and our men. After my messenger delivers it he will turn around and come right back so we would know that the message got through.

Then I ordered the archers among my guards to pick off any of the Earl's men who are foolish enough to get within range of their longbows.

And I must admit that I did suggest in the message I sent to William that killing the Earl and his brother might be an opportunity for us. I hope William agrees. If fighting starts, and it almost certainly will, it will not end until either Lord Baldwin and his moron brother are dead or we are.

It could be a good thing, Lord Baldwin and his brother being dead I mean—Baldwin's castle at Restormel and his Earldom may be available if he is gone and we move quickly.

******

The next very day Sir Ralph got tired of waiting and played the fool despite my warning. He arrogantly trotted his horse around the muddy pond and right up to the wall on the north side of the keep.

"What is Lady Dorothy's decision?" he demanded as he looked up to where I was standing at an archer's slit on the curtain wall. He was sitting on his horse not ten feet below me.

I knew her decision because we had talked about her alternatives ever since the Earl and his brother first proposed the marriage. We had become quite close, Lady Dorothy and I. I had even shared a few of our plans for George and assured her the Earl of Cornwall and his men were no match for William and his archers.

So I delivered her message myself—I shot an arrow straight down into the arrogant Norman's upturned face. *I was not always a priest you know.*

The sight of his stupid brother falling off his horse seemed to really piss off the Earl.

A few moments later there was a great hue and cry as Baldwin and his men surged forward towards the castle walls waving their swords. And then they got to the walls and looked up to find a dozen or more defenders firing arrows and dropping rocks down on them.

They quickly turned around and ran the other way leaving Sir Ralph and more bodies on the ground and crawling away. The damn fools had even forgotten to bring ladders.

Baldwin and his men left soon thereafter, but not before they worked themselves into a rage and started to attack the handful of hovels in the castle's village.

They began by torching one of them and cutting down a couple of villagers who had not been smart enough to run when the fighting started at the castle.

But then the Earl stopped them. Apparently it suddenly dawned on the Norman fool that his men were destroying some of the very property he wanted to add to his own estate.

In any event, Baldwin and his men missed most of Trematon's people because just about every one of them was either in the fields helping to bring in the harvest or inside the castle with Lady Dorothy and her children.

In the end, after standing around thinking about the situation for a while, the Earl left Sir Ralph and the rest of his dead next to the castle walls and went home with his men to get reinforcements and beat his wife or whatever it is that nobles do when they do not get what they want.

We buried them without prayers three days later when they began to smell.

We would almost certainly see the Earl of Cornwall and his men again when his harvest was in and more of his retainers are available. There was not much time to lose. As soon as the Earl and his men were out of sight I used one of the castle's two horses to send yet another messenger to William—this one to describe what had happened and suggest some precautionary steps he might want to take.

******

While I waited for William's response I spent my time counselling and consoling Lady Dorothy and her daughters—and composing messages and parchments to take to Prince John and the papal nuncio. *It is always best to be prepared.*

Chapter Three

Reinforcements are summoned.

Thomas's second message reached me while I was drilling the men on how to respond to attacks by mounted knights and men at arms using the newfangled bladed pikes Brian had begun producing for the Company before we left Cyprus.

It was quite an encouraging message: Thomas thinks Baldwin has gone to his Restormel Castle and will return to Trematon with more of his men right after the harvest is in.

My brother is right as usual—catching the Earl out of his castle and killing him if he gives us cause is just too good of an opportunity for us to pass up.

I sent the messenger back on a fresh horse, newly acquired and the only one we had left, to tell Thomas we would be coming.

Two hours later the archers and I were marching along the cart path to Trematon. We started quickly because I had already had the horse carts loaded with the supplies we might need and most of the coin chests—and sent rest of our coin chests to be loaded on our galleys. George and the boys in Thomas's little school came with us.

I thought about putting George and the boys on to one of our galleys to keep them out of harm's way but decided I could better keep my eye on them and keep them safer if they came with us.

Once Harold has the galleys loaded, and they should be by now, all he will have to do to protect them is push them out into the water with a handful of men on each to act as its guards.

Having the galleys already loaded and ready to sail means all Harold and his men will need to do is untie them and let them drift down to the safety of Falmouth's harbour if the Earl surprises us and attacks here at our camp instead of at Trematon.

******

One thing the Earl's behaviour accomplished was to make up my mind as to where we should spend the winter. Our camp along the river and Trematon Castle are going to be our bases at least until the spring. After that, who knows?

Our galleys will stay anchored in the shallows of the River Fal with a small guard of sailors under Harold's command until we know it is safe to once again pull them back ashore. The cogs, of course, will have to stay anchored near the mouth of the river where now until we decide to move them elsewhere.

In essence, what I decided was to have everyone except Harold and the sailors on our boats go with me to Trematon to relieve Thomas and Edmund's widow. We would send the horse carts back to get more supplies from the boats if it looked like we might need them.

The only other thing weighing on my mind before I set out for Trematon was Sir Percy. Right after Thomas' second messenger arrived with his message Sir Percy trotted into camp on his horse leading another horse carrying his shield and all his armour.

"Hello Hello" he said as he slid off his horse and held out his hand with a friendly smile.

"I have come to say goodbye. I have been summoned to the Earl's muster. Well we all have been summoned, have not we? The Earl's knights I mean. All five us from Cornwall and our men who are in the village levies. Probably two hundred or so in all I would think."

"Not that I have many men to contribute to the Earl's army, mind you. Just Otto. But I sent him straight away to Restormel Castle to tell the Earl I would be coming. Yes I did. I have no choice in the matter, do I?"

"What is happening, Sir Percy? Why the muster?" *I know damn well why the Earl is mustering his men. And Sir Percy knows I know.*

"Why Lord Edmund's widow has flummoxed him has not she? He was going to marry his brother to her in order to get his hands on her castle, but somehow he got himself killed instead of married. Damn shame, of course." *He is trying to warn me and Thomas without betraying his vassalage.*

"It could be dangerous for the Earl, could not it? Edmund's widow's has a lot of friends, does she?"

"Oh aye. She does. She certainly does. But Baldwin's full of himself and he has got a lot of men in his manors even though almost all of them are churls. Most of them are not real soldiers, of course, just serfs and churls. It will probably go badly for us. Probably be another Hattin I would think."

"Well then. Why do you go? Why not just stay in Falmouth and let the Earl fight it out with the widow's friends without you?"

"I cannot do that. Honour you know. My wife wanted a place to settle down so I gave the Earl my word. Probably should not have pledged my liege to the Earl to be the sheriff hereabouts but I did. Be the death of me I suppose, but there you are?"

"Would you excuse me for one moment, Sir Percy? There is a matter I must attend to." .....

"Harold, Harold come over here for a minute will you please? I want you to meet a friend of ours, a very good friend."

"Sir Percy, this is Harold from Lewes. He is the sergeant captain of all of our sailors and he will be wintering right here in Falmouth with our galleys and cogs."

"Harold, this is my friend Sir Percy. We are good friends even though he is the Earl's sheriff in Falmouth."

The men smiled at each other as they shook hands.

"Do you know how to swim Sir Percy?" I asked the elderly knight—who was clearly as baffled as Harold by my question. "No? Well that is good, very good actually."

Then the faces of both men showed surprise, a great deal of surprise, when I told Harold what I wanted him to do next.

"Harold. We are taking Sir Percy as a prisoner and holding him for ransom as an honoured guest. I want you to immediately take him out to one of our cogs and hold him there while we are gone.

"You are to keep it anchored in the harbour at all times and on no account is Sir Percy to be allowed ashore for any reason until either Thomas or I return—and on no account is he to be bound or in any way mistreated. To the contrary, I want you to put him in the forward castle with warm bedding and make sure he gets all the food and drink he wants."

I will give Harold much more detailed instructions about Sir Percy in a few minutes when we are alone—we do not kill or mistreat our friends.

"Oh yes, I forgot; Henry, please send a messenger to Sir Percy's wife assuring her he is alive and well and will stay that way. Tell her Sir Percy will be returned to her all safe and sound as soon as the matter is resolved between Edmund's widow and the Earl."

******

Dividing one's forces is never a good idea so all of our men except the sailors with Harold are accompanying the supplies and coin chests we are taking to Trematon.

If Baldwin and his men come this way they will find our camp deserted and all our boats in the river; we are taking everything else with us except the spare weapons and the amphorae filled with grain and other foodstuffs we still have on our galleys and cogs. They will be safe on them while we are away and so will Sir Percy.

I thought about leaving more of our coin chests with Harold but finally decided against it. *Best to keep such things close, yes it is.*

George and the two boys from Falmouth being learnt with him are riding on the first wagon and taking everything in with big eyes. They will fall asleep in about an hour if the past is any guide.

It took almost four days for our column to reach Trematon. We did not need to hurry because we kept receiving messengers from Thomas telling us the Earl was still assembling his army at Restormel.

One reason it took so long is that every day we stopped several times along the way to practice such things as what we would do if our convoy was suddenly attacked and how we would face the Earl's army and manoeuvre about it if we have time to get organized.

And since every man was carrying a bow in addition to his other weapons, every training session ended with an archery tournament with a silver coin for the winner and a copper coin for the second.

The tournaments did not delay us at all—the men shot their arrows as they walked past their targets and then a working party from among our apprentice archers picked everything up and threw it on the last wagon. They also herded the livestock we bought but had not yet killed.

Our targets were the sheep we cooked and ate at the end of each day—and paid too much for because we wanted the local serfs and churls to be friendly and assist us in any way they can in the coming battle with Earl Baldwin and thereafter.

It seems to be working; I do not know how they learnt of it but by the end of the second day the serfs and churls living near the cart path to Trematon were bringing sheep and cattle to us in the hope we would buy them and use them as targets. *To my surprise there were no franklins holding their own lands along the way. No wonder Cornwall is so poor.*

It was not just the walking and the make-believe war practicing that made us so slow. It was the carts and wagons carrying our arrow bales and coin chests and other supplies.

Since we had no horses it was the men themselves who were pulling the wagons and horse carts—and making fun of each other and complaining about it as they did. As every commander knows it was a very encouraging sign to hear our archers loudly complaining and teasing each other about being used as horses and such. It really was; if they had been truly unhappy they would have been surly and secretive. The lack of rain to wet them and the unlimited amount of good meat undoubtedly helped.

I thought about taking Sir Percy's two horses but quickly decided against it. Instead I had one of our man take them to Falmouth with a ransom note and a suggestion that his wife send the note to the Earl straightaway; taking things from the local people is not the reputation we want to have—and there is no need to get Sir Percy in trouble with the Earl if we fail to kill him and take his place.

Even the blown horse ridden in by Thomas' last messenger was not being used. It still needed some time to recover from its hard ride so it was being walked by Raymond a couple of miles ahead of us. I was confident Raymond would only mount it and ride back to sound the alarm if he saw a danger we needed to know about.

Raymond is one of the original archers and among the most dependable of all our men; I was confident he would know danger if he saw it and immediately warn us. He was also one of the few archers who knew horses; so I was also confident he would not ride it before it was ready to be ridden. *He does not know it yet but we are going to have a force of mounted archers and he is going to command them.*

Several dozen of our men were under Raymond's direct command during our march to Trematon. He and the horse walked on the rough cart path about a mile ahead of us and his men walked in a long line that stretched out for a mile or more on either side of him. He also had a couple of men walking far out on either side of our column and behind us too.

I did not know anything about the Earl of Cornwall's military experience and ability so I was taking precautions against him being competent. Some of my men are not fully trained yet to fight on land and I was determined we will not be taken by a surprise attack.

Trematon came in sight late in the morning of the fourth day of our march. I sent my main column to the north under Martin while I continued on to the castle with some of the supply carts and about a hundred men who would join the castle's defenders.

Thomas was right. Trematon is not very defensible— unless it has a big force inside its walls as it soon will have.

******

Thomas saw us coming and rode out to meet me on one of Trematon's two horses. And the very first thing he did when we walked together into Trematon's bailey was introduce me and George to Lord Edmund's widow and the two bashful little girls who hid behind her and peered out from behind her sheepskin skirts.

"Lady Dorothy, this is my brother William I have told you so much about. And that little fellow there is his son George. George's four friends are Roger and Cyrus from Falmouth and Andreas and Augustus from Cyprus. They are being learned to scribe and sum with George as I think I mentioned to you."

It is fun to watch the young ones shyly peek at each other and try to pretend they are not. They are all quite curious about each other it seems. Even Lady Dorothy noticed it and smiled. So did Thomas and I.

Our supply and treasure wagons were pulled into the castle's little bailey. The sheep and cattle we bought along the way for targets and provisions, on the other hand, stayed with the main column for food.

If we have enough time we will herd some of the sheep and cattle into the bailey for the castle's use. But even without them we have brought enough grain inside the castle walls for its defenders to hold out for many months— if there is enough firewood for cooking the bread. *Which it turned out there was not.*

We will decide tomorrow where our main body of archers should be located. The important thing for now is to keep them far enough away from the castle so the Earl's spies and gallopers, if he has any and is smart enough to send them, would not be able to see them and warn him that he is walking into a trap.

Raymond immediately mounted our horse and trotted off with one of the local men running alongside. The local man would be his guide and the two of them will join the gallopers with our other horses where Thomas has placed them as "lookers" watching for the Earl.

The lookers are watching the river ford everyone seems to think the Earl's forces will have to use if he leads his men west from Restormel towards either Trematon or our camp along the River Fal. Their job is to lie low and watch the crossing—and send gallopers to tell us when the Earl's men reach it and which way they head after they wade across.

All the rest of our men who walked into Trematon with me, about eighty in all and mostly archers, jammed themselves into the castle's little bailey along with the horse carts and began the usual chores of campaign life—setting up tents, digging shite holes, and collecting water from the brook nearest the castle walls.

They did so under Thomas' watchful eye—he is big on keeping piss and shite out of the water and away from the camp. He claims the book he read at the monastery said the Romans kept them apart and their empire lasted for almost a thousand years. *I am not sure I have ever really understood the connection.*

******

It did not take long to get the men in the castle organized and out of sight with a sergeant appointed as the master sergeant to keep them that way. Then Thomas and I took the castle's two horses and rode out to inspect the surrounding area.

We were looking for the best place to locate the rest of our men, the ones who continued on to the north when I walked into the castle with the others. Some of the nearby woodlands looked quite promising as places where we might be able to conceal our men—and from which we might be able to launch a massive surprise attack on the Earl's army after his men begin their attack on Trematon.

Massive surprise attacks with more and better men and weapons are almost always the best way to defeat an enemy. At least that is what I always thought and it probably says in the Bible. The problem, of course, is fooling your enemy so he goes along with your plan. Hopefully the Earl of Cornwall is as stupid as Thomas described him to be.

After Thomas and I rode around a bit we dismounted and stood in an open area next to one of the woodlands. From up there we could see the castle and the lands surrounding it. It was time to talk about how we were going to proceed when the Earl arrives with his army.

I suggested perhaps we might have our men inside castle put up a token resistance and then retreat into the keep—and let the Earl's men into the bailey. Then when they are all inside we could use our larger force of men to surround the castle so the Earl and his men are trapped in the bailey without food and water. Alternately, I suggested, we could abandon Trematon entirely and then lay a siege on the castle as soon as the Earl and his men enter it.

Thomas did not like either idea. He said he had read a really old parchment book about Rome in the monastery describing just such a battle—and how the men who retreated into the keep lost their lives even though their allies came and surrounded the men who had surrounded them.

According to Thomas, the Romans trapped one enemy force inside the walls of a fortress by building their own wall

all the way around it—and then built a second wall facing in the other direction to keep out the relieving force of their allies who came to free their friends.

The relief force was not successful. The Romans held both walls until many of the people inside the fortress starved to death. The rest then surrendered at which point the would-be relievers gave up and went home because there was no one left to rescue.

After thinking and talking about it I had to agree with Thomas. Luring the Earl's force into Trematon and then surrounding it might be a good idea for some castles, but probably not for Trematon and certainly not for us.

Later I decided the idea of letting the Earl of Cornwall into Trematon and then laying a siege on him was one of the dumbest ideas I had ever had. We needed to bring the Earl's army to battle quickly and kill him so we can take over his castle and get back to recruiting and training archers.

******

We adopted a different plan—Thomas will hold the castle and I would lead the men in a charging run out of the trees and take the Earl and his men in the rear as soon as they spread his out to surround the castle and begin their attack. Since we would be on foot with a couple of miles to run it will take us about fifteen minutes to get there.

It should work for it means Thomas and his men will only have to hold Trematon for about fifteen minutes—and it is virtually certain Trematon can be held for such a short period of time since we already have more than enough fighting men inside the castle to hold its walls against the Earl's untrained men and then sortie out to defeat them even if I never begin my surprise attack.

Of course we have a lot of men in the castle; my son is in there and so is my brother and most of the coins we had earned in the Holy Land.

What we decided to do if the Earl and his men do not quickly surround the castle and launch a major attack is creep out of the trees in the dark like thieves and storm into the Earl's encampment at dawn. I will make the decision after I see where and how the Earl sets up his camp and how his men are disbursed and behave.

Whatever we do, Thomas and I agree, we must do everything possible to kill Baldwin while he is outside his own castle and vulnerable. Otherwise we will have to lay siege to his castle at Restormel and his vassals and his relatives and friends, if he has any, might be able to come and relieve him.

In any event, by the time the sun went down Thomas and I had decided to hide me and a large force of our men here in the trees and for me to lead them against the Earl's army as soon as it spreads out and surrounds the castle. It means I would be leading an attack on the Earl's army with all the men who continued northward whilst Thomas was leading the smaller party of men and some of the wagons into the castle.

There is another stand of trees where we might hide closer to the castle but it is too close— the Earl's men might come across our men when they go out searching for firewood for their cooking fires.

Once the decision was made we rode back to the castle to have dinner with Lady Dorothy and the children. I hope it is not roast mutton again. I know Lady Dorothy and her tenants have a lot of sheep but I am getting tired of mutton after five days of eating the archers' targets.

I would ride north in the morning and lead the waiting men to their new positions.

******

Early the next morning, after a fine evening of conversation and a meal of mutton stew and onions, Thomas and I used Trematon's two horses to ride north for about an hour to meet Martin and the men who will be in the trees as our ambush force. We found them camping beside a little stream that runs into the River Fal below the ford.

Martin called the sergeants together as soon as we arrived and I briefly explained the situation as soon as they gathered around. Then we led them and their men on a march to the thick woodland where we would wait in hiding until the Earl arrives with his men.

We reached the woods about noon and Thomas and I immediately began talking with Martin and his sergeants while the men made a camp next to the little brook that runs through the trees. The woods was thick and wet and filled with biting bugs but it would do.

The first thing we did was walk out and assemble all the sergeants on the little hill between the trees and Trematon. From there I could point out landmarks to them and explain what we are going to do and why and when.

It is important Martin and his sergeants understand what we are going to do and why and where we are going to do it—it will be them and their men I would be leading out of the woods when the Earl and his men begin their attack on the castle.

We will launch our attack, I told them, either when the Earl's men begin their attack or, if the Earl and his men immediately settle in for a siege, on their camp at the dawn's early light on the first morning after they arrive. Either way, Martin and the sergeants and the chosen men who are their seconds need to know what to do and who to follow if Martin or I go down.

"Okay. Everyone listen up. That is Trematon Castle over there. It is going to be attacked by the Earl of Cornwall and some of his men in a couple of days. He is a newly arrived Norman lord who wants to evict the widow of the Company's friend, Lord Robert, and her two young daughters who live there and add it to his lands east of here."

"And he is pretty stupid in addition to being greedy. He thinks the castle is weak and only defended by the woman and a dozen or so of her people of whom not a one is a real fighting man. He does not know the castle now has almost a hundred of our men inside its walls."

"We do not know how strong a force the Earl will bring or whether he will attack or just try to starve them out. But since he only thinks he will only be fighting a dozen or so untrained men it is likely he will attack when he finds she will not let him in. Then there will be a fight where we will not only outnumber and surprise the bastards but our men will also be much better trained and more experienced."

Which is always how it is best to fight. When you have got the enemy at a great weakness, I mean.

"What the Earl also does not know is a hundred or so of our men, and my son George and his little friends, are already inside the castle under Bishop Thomas's command. He also does not know all the rest of us will be waiting here in the woods to fall upon his rear after he starts his attack." *At least that is the plan.*

"And here is how we are going to do it."

After two hours of explaining and pointing and answering questions I was beginning to lose my voice but fairly confident the sergeants and their seconds understand enough of what we are going to do to explain it to their men.

"So now we are going to go back to your men and explain things to them and begin practicing. This afternoon we will simulate a charge against a force at the Trematon walls and then early tomorrow morning we will move out of our camp in the dark so we can practice an early morning attack against an enemy camp in the early light of dawn."

"But before you go back to your men and explain what we are going to do, you also need to know what to tell them not to do—they are not to wander out of our camp or to light any fires and or show any smoke during the day. They are also to be absolute quiet and only talk in whispers when we are forming up for our attack whenever it might be.

"And know this. It is important to the success of our attack that no one is seen by the Earl's spies or peasants they might chat up on their march to get here. We do not want to lose any of our men because someone does something stupid. So it is on every sergeant's head that his men never let themselves be seen and do all their cooking in the middle of the night—so the smoke is never see and is totally gone by the time the sun comes up."

"And one more thing when we fight it is important every one of your men is wearing his sailor's cap and either carrying a bow or a bladed pike—it is the only way the rest of us and our men in the castle will know who is a friend and who is not."

We really need something so our men can identify each other in the confusion of a battle. Maybe a coloured tunic or cap?

******

After our session with Martin and his sergeants, Thomas and I rode back to Trematon for a dinner of mutton and onions. Afterwards I walked with Martin back to his camp. Starting tonight I will begin sleeping in the woods with our men until the Earl and his men show up.

And, of course, Thomas and I are doing a number of other things to make sure the Earl and his men receive an especially warm welcome—such as putting out gallopers on his likely route so we would know when he was coming and who he was bringing with him.

Also, and even though we did not tell the sergeants because they did not need to know, we scattered half a dozen or so of our new archer apprentices in the empty village and around in the outlying fields to pose as the village's shepherds and farm workers. They were needed to make things look normal even though the sheep had either been herded away to safety in the north or into the bailey to be eaten in the event the Earl's attack turned into a siege.

The arrogant sonofabitch is not going to sneak up on us and surprise us if I can help it. Not with my son and brother in the castle.

******

A galloper just arrived on a blown horse after a brief stop at the castle to sound the alarm—Raymond had sent him in to report that a force of several hundred armed men had been seen coming out of Devon. They were approaching the River Tamar ford when the galloper started out and was almost certainly in Cornwall by the time he reached us.

Another blown horse? Our horses are really very poor; they have no bottom do they?

The result of his warning at Trematon, the galloper told me with a big smile when I inquired, was a lot of running around and shouting sergeants.

Several hours later a second galloper arrived—the Earl and his army are taking the footpath towards Trematon—and he is bringing a little over two hundred of his men with him. *Hmm; that is quite a few to deal with the dozen or so men he thinks are inside with Lady Dorothy.*

According to the second messenger the Earl's men are carrying many long ladders on horse carts and he is at least two days away at the slow speed they are moving. None of his men split off to go on the cart path which runs towards our training camp and Falmouth.

It sounds safe enough since the Earl is at least a day away so I decided to walk in to Trematon with a squad of men. I wanted to see what is going on at the castle and I wanted to talk to Thomas to make sure we were in agreement as to how we would each respond to various possibilities.

We did not want any unnecessary casualties so it was important for Thomas to once again remind his men everyone coming out of the trees would be wearing a sailor's cap and carrying either a long bladed pike or a bow.

Another reason I decided to walk in, truth to tell, is that I was getting tired of eating fire-blackened mutton with the men.

And it is a good thing I did, walk in to the castle I mean. Thomas promised he would once again warn every man in the castle not to shoot or stab or drop rocks on our own men. He did not actually admit it, but I think he had forgotten to mention it to them.

Then, before I walked back to the Company's camp in the woods, Thomas and I, and George and his little friends, had a delicious dinner of mutton stew with Lady Dorothy and her daughters. She was greatly relieved and thankful when she found out George and his friends and Thomas would be staying in the castle with her and her children.

I am really getting tired of eating mutton at every meal although the bread and onions were very good indeed. The cheese, however, was quite questionable—I had the runs right after we ate. At least I think it was the cheese.

After dinner I led my little company of men back to the woods where we would spend the night. It did not look as though the Earl and his men would arrive until the day after tomorrow but I wanted the men to once again practice attacking a sleeping camp just as dawn's early light comes up over the horizon in the morning.

Yesterday morning's practice attack did not go very well and this time we will go for another of the likely places where the Earl might pitch his camp.

******

We had been getting periodic reports from Raymond's gallopers as to the location of the Earl and his men. So it was no surprise at all this afternoon when a disorganized mass of men came over the little hill to our east and started down towards the castle.

A few minutes later we watched from just inside the tree line as a small party of eight or nine mounted men appeared behind the walking men. Undoubtedly it was the

Earl and the seven knights who held Cornwall's knight fees. Why they were bringing up the rear instead of leading surprised me.

In any event, Sir Percy was right—the Earl had called all of the knights and their men in from their knight's fees even though their harvests were almost certainly not all in. Well not all of his knights, of course—I had Sir Percy tucked away with Harold on one of our boats.

Except for the Earl and his men everything was very quiet and nothing was moving except for some deer nibbling on tree branches as they drifted past our camp.

From here in the woods I could just make out the castle. The gate was closed and the drawbridge over the pond was up. The place looked deserted. And that is the way it should look because yesterday the sheep and the castle's serfs and churls were all moved more than a half day's walk from the castle and our fake shepherds and village residents recalled.

The village looked empty too. It should; it was empty. The villagers were good half day's walk on the far side of the castle so they should be safe as well. Besides, the Earl wants to own them so he is not likely to kill them.

Our men seemed almost glad to see the Earl and his men. Probably because it meant the waiting was over—as every soldier can tell you, it is the waiting before the battle starts that grinds you down because you start thinking of all the terrible things that might happen.

In any event our men got all excited and curious. They all started talking and moving towards the edge of the trees to get a better look. A few sharp words from the sergeants moved them back to where they belong and out of sight in the trees.

We cannot allow our men to look no matter how careful they might be—we do not want to take the chance of someone being seen and ruining our ambush. Then more of our men would then be likely to get hurt or killed before we finish them off, the Earl and his men that is.

The immediate question we faced is what Baldwin would do now he has arrived—attempt to parley with the castle to see if Lady Dorothy has changed her mind? Pitch a camp and organize an attack? Or charge right in and have a go at the castle?

I doubt he is going to approach the castle for a parley after what happened to his stupid brother but you never can be sure with these hereditary lords whose families came over from France. They have got weak blood you know.

Ah well, we will soon find out soon enough.

******

As we watched from the tree line we could see Baldwin's men putting down the loads they were carrying and beginning to gather around the Earl and his little group of horsemen. *At least I think that is Baldwin; I hope so.*

After a few minutes a mounted knight rode towards the castle with a man running next to him. The two men stopped well short of the wall. The knight must have heard what happened to the Earl's brother when he rode all the way up to it.

Now what is he doing? Of course, I bet the man's blowing a horn to get the castle's intention. Well, I would wager he has already got it but I suppose the formalities have to be observed. Richard is a stickler for such things but the rumours we have heard say John is not.

I wondered what the knight was saying and if Thomas was going to reply. Thomas told me he was going to keep the castle totally silent and hope someone gets careless and comes within range.

It happens, you know. The heralds think they are not being heard because they are too far away so they come closer. I got a Saracen that way for Lord Edmund. My arrow caught the wind and stuck him in the throat. Probably the best shot I ever made.

****** *Thomas*

From where we stood up behind the battlements of the keep my sergeants and I could see more and more of the Earl's men gathering on the little hill in front of the castle. It looked like they are being pushed into some kind of line as we watched. And we could see they were carrying ladders, lots of ladders.

I knew it would not be long now and we were as ready as we could be. It was time for my sergeants and me to go back to the battlements on the castle's curtain wall to stand with our men.

As I waved and smiled at Lady Dorothy and started down the narrow winding stone stairs I started wondering once again if Baldwin will lead his men in the attack or just order them in and watch from a safe distance.

Our plan is for my men here in the castle to put up the weakest possible defence needed to keep the Earl's men out until the Earl himself comes close enough to be shot for a poacher's goose. That is why we acted as if we were only a few.

Making sure everyone waited for the Earl to come close was one of the reasons I went up on the wall to be with the archers waiting at the arrow slits—to make sure everyone stayed with the plan and did not reveal himself too early. Another was to once again remind everyone once again our men who will all be coming out of the woods wearing sailors' caps and carrying either longbows or bladed pikes.

Motivating the men to do the right thing is important. I had thought about promising a gold bezant coin to whoever kills the Earl. But I finally decided not to offer it because it would probably cause almost everyone to push out their arrows at an extreme range in hopes of getting lucky—and that might cause Baldwin to hang back.

What I did instead was offer a prize of five copper coins for each ladder pushed away with a man on it and two silver coins for every man who kills an attacker who gets over the castle wall. Once the fighting starts I will be constantly reminding the archers of those prizes, of that you can be sure. *I will also begin offering some coins for anyone who pushes an arrow into Baldwin once he gets close enough.*

William was undoubtedly watching and would decide when his men should attack and hit Baldwin's army in the rear. But just in case I put a couple of my steadiest men up at one of the tower windows with a flag and a candle lantern. I will have them waved if I need William to launch an immediate attack for any reason.

George and the boys and Lady Dorothy and her children are up there too. I was not taking any chances.

****** *William*

Things were tense out here in the trees. The mounted knight and his horn blower had returned and are talking to the group of mounted men. One of them must be Earl Baldwin. Oh. Now what? Yes. Here they come. But why so few?

A small group of men was moving forward. Of course. They have probably been ordered to go forward and see if the castle was as abandoned and undefended as it appeared to be. They were all carrying shields and two or three of them seemed to be carrying a ladder.

About ten men cautiously walked up to the lowest spot on Trematon's north wall and placed the ladder against it. A man started to slowly climb the ladder with his shield up. Then something happened and we watched as the ladder slowly tipped over and he fell to the ground waving his arms and dropping his shield.

The men at the wall start to run but then they stopped and came back.

Of course! I bet someone reached out of one of the archers' slits with one of the long bladed pikes Thomas asked us to bring him and pushed the ladder over. They have got a notch between the blade and the staff that is just right to do it.

In a few seconds three or four of the men in the Earl's advance party were standing around the man who fell and trying to get him on his feet. The rest of the Earl's men were once again just standing around next to the wall.

Interestingly enough, no one had his shield up or was acting alarmed particularly alarmed. There must have been no arrows or shouts from the inside—they probably think is it a servant or someone trying to keep them out by pushing the ladder over.

After a minute or so a rider detached himself from Baldwin's party and rode towards the men standing next to the wall. He must be shouting some kind of order for once again the men started putting up the ladder. This time they were going to try a little further down the wall.

And once again something happened and the ladder fell over when the man on the ladder got close to the top. And once again the men gathered around the fallen man without raising their shields.

At this point the rider trotted a little closer. Then he dismounted and walked to the wall. The way he was standing looked like he was shouting something up to the people in the castle.

After a while, he turned back and remounted his horse and slowly trotted back to Baldwin. The men by the wall started to follow him. They did not get very far.

The rider turned his head and said something to them over his shoulder as he trotted away. They turned and walked back to the wall. The man who went down on the second ladder was still on the ground next to the wall. From what we could see from up here on the hill he did not appear to be moving.

There was a brief conversation when the rider reached the party of mounted men and I could make out arms being waved about. Then several of the mounted men wheeled away and a few seconds later all Baldwin's men begin slowly walking toward to the castle walls.

The Earl and his little party of mounted men were right behind them. We could see the banners fluttering on their lances as their horses trotted forward. The damn fools were getting ready to charge at the castle wall as if they are at some kind of tournament.

"Get ready, but hold fast until the order is given. It is not yet time to move." I shouted with my loudest voice.

All along our line of men in the trees my order was repeated by the sergeants. Wait. *Almost. Wait for it.*

Baldwin's men were carrying several dozen or more ladders, maybe a lot more. That was actually pretty smart because it meant there would be more climbers than defenders so that some of the climbers might be able to get over the wall—if there were only a few defenders as Baldwin apparently believed.

In what seemed like only an instant the great mass of the Earl's men moved forward and spread out all along the base of the castle wall. Then some command must have been given for almost simultaneously all the ladders went up and men began slowly and cautiously climbing them. All the men on the ladders with shields had them up.

Less than half of the Earl's men appear to be carrying shields but Thomas' men must still be waiting—the Earl's men who were not climbing still do not have their shields raised. And once again the ladders began to go over as the climbers got close to the top.

Then it happened. In a trice an absolute stream of arrows and rocks began to pour from ramparts on to the Earl's men gathered below along the castle wall. I could not see the arrows and rocks come down at this distance, of course, but I could certainly see the sudden reaction of the men who were receiving them.

A lot of the arrows on the north side seem to be being directed at the Earl and his horse—I think that was what was happening because there seemed to be a particularly great amount of confusion in the area where Baldwin and his knights had been sitting on their horses. Most of the riders' horses were down or staggering except for one running off without a rider. All the men at the walls with shields have them up.

"Attack," I shouted as loudly as I could as I pointed my longbow toward the castle and the men around it. "Attack."

Then I started running towards the castle.

We burst out of the trees as a great mass of disorganized men and began running towards the battle that was going on all along the wall of castle in front of us. There were a few shouts from our men but they soon ended as we began trotting towards the castle.

We had practiced this before and we knew we needed to save our breaths for the run and the fighting that will follow. At least, praise the Lord, it looks as though we will significantly outnumber the castle's attackers and, even better, catch them spread out and unready to receive us.

******

I was moving well and most of my men were staying up with me. That was good because we want to crash into the Baldwin's men in one great irresistible mass. Like everyone else I was wearing a sailor's cap and carrying a little shield in addition to my bow and two quivers; one with longs and one with heavies.

A couple of our men were way out in front of us. They were clearly racing each other to be the first to engage. They must have very good legs and very small memories because they were moving ahead despite the orders to move together and spread out. And as I looked back I could see a few of our men lagging behind.

Damn. Another mistake. I should have placed a steady man back there to chivvy them along and take the names and kick the arses of those who were deliberately avoiding the fight. Their futures are going to be very dim if I can identify them.

Generally, however, things were going well. At least so far. Our men were following their sergeants and spreading out as they moved towards the castle. That was good because our plan was to sweep around the castle and the men at its walls like the horns of the ox—so the men gathered at the castle wall were inside the horns and could not escape, particularly the Earl.

Unlike Thomas who told me he intended to wait until the last moment so Baldwin is not warned away. I had already put a bounty on him—ten silver coins for the man who kills him.

My men and I were still some distance from the castle and moving fast when the Earl's men began to see us and become alarmed. Our arrival was obviously unexpected and they did not know what to do.

The indecision of Baldwin's men did not last very long. One after another they began to scatter and run. Some of them even ran soon enough and fast enough to get away before the horns of our attack closed around them. A few foolish souls even turned around as if they were going to stand and fight. But then they too began to run.

Among the early runners attempting to escape were a couple of knights in armour who had not dismounted or were somehow able to quickly swing themselves back on board their horses. One of them galloped away safely through the shower of arrows and rocks falling on the crowd of panic-stricken men, but the horse of the other suddenly went down and sent him tumbling.

I was puffing and had a pain in my side by the time I finally reached the pile of dead and wounded men on the ground where I had last seen the Earl and his mounted retinue. And there he was; Baldwin was in the middle of a pile of men and horses on the ground—deader than a plucked chicken in the cook's pot.

He was seriously dead and there was no half way about it. Thomas obviously had every archer shoot at Baldwin as soon the fighting started and keep shooting.

Baldwin's armour did not save him—he and his horse and the ground and men and horses closest around him have the arrows of our longbow men sticking out of them everywhere. The metal tips of our "heavies" will go through chain mail you know. Baldwin and his horse looked like one of those little cushions with pins in it I saw in the Damascus market years ago.

Thomas' archers obviously continued to shoot at the Earl long after he died. Of course they did. Thomas wanted to make sure of him so he obviously did what he told me he intended to do—lead our best archers to where the Baldwin was approaching the wall and shout out a promise of a silver coin for every arrow or bolt he pulls out of the Earl or his horse.

No doubt some of the shafts were from Thomas himself, but there were so many others that was likely some of the men will get a good handful of coins. *And worth every penny of it.*

We have got the result we wanted and there was no doubt about it—Cornwall was going to need a new Earl.

"Stop killing them. Take prisoners" …. "Stop killing. Take prisoners."

******

Thomas waved down to me from the castle ramparts and a few minutes later the castle gate opened. He came out with some of his men and a big grin on his face.

He was very excited and had an urge to talk as we shook hands and clapped each other on the shoulder. All the men around us were as excited as he was and so was I. Everyone was talking at once.

"Well we got the bugger did not we?"

"Aye. That we did, Thomas. That we did."

"Well then. Let us see to the prisoners. Are you still going to let them go home if they pledge their liege to you? I hope so. First thing tomorrow I will say prayers over all the dead, theirs and ours and then I will go with you to Restormel Castle."

And that was what we did.

******

Our review of the battle was not pretty as we walked together and talked in the evening after we had eaten a victory meal and enjoyed more than a few bowls of ale. We made a lot of mistakes and we knew it. Thomas called me to task on several of them and rightly so.

"We won big but we were damn lucky to do so. What if Baldwin had kept his wits and had a reserve come in behind us once you had spread out your men and commenced your attack? We would have been the ones slaughtered."

"Or what if he had crossed the river somewhere else and he had showed up before I had time to send for you? Or what if he had trained his men so they had turned from the castle walls and faced your wild charge in a steady formation?"

"Aye, Thomas. You are right. We took some big risks and I made a really big mistake by not covering the lesser crossings and holding back a reserve force. And we should have had more spies and horsemen out there to warn us in case Baldwin came another way."

"And more horses; we should have had many more horses and much better horses, so we could move our men about faster."

"Well done is done my priestly brother. Though you are right—we were lucky the Earl was more inept than I was, God rest his useless soul. Now what?" *And right then and there I swore to myself that I would spend more time thinking behind my eyes before I sent my men into battle in the future. It was an important decision.*

"Why now we get ourselves off to Restormel Castle and help John and Richard find a new lord for Cornwall and perhaps a new bishop for the county as well."

Chapter Four

On to Restormel.

Thomas and I saw to both our wounded and those of the Earl, and then we moved around from campfire to campfire joking with our men as they began celebrating their victory by roasting sheep from those of Trematon's flock inside the bailey.

Everyone except the wounded and dead were either excited or unhappy or both—happy for our resounding victory and unhappy because in the morning many of the men would be going with us to the late Earl's seat at Restormel Castle.

After the sun went down Thomas and I had a second and very private victory dinner in the castle with Lady Dorothy and the equally excited children. We had been promised a celebration supper of lamb chops and new cheese. They were delicious.

By noon the next day the dead were buried with the proper words and Thomas and I were on horses and riding towards Restormel Castle. We were at the head of a column of several hundred of our men. A number of horse wagons carrying our tents and unused supplies were travelling on the rough and rarely used cart path with us. Some of them, unfortunately, were being pulled by our men because we did not have enough horses.

Not all of our men are marching in our column, of course; a goodly number are remaining at Trematon to guard the castle and our prisoners and care for the wounded.

It was an interesting trip along a well-worn footpath and several times we saw men running across the fields and through the woods. They were probably escapees from the Earl's defeated army who were trying to get back home.

We paid them no mind and wished them well. Indeed, a few of them actually came to us and joined our column when we happily shouted and waved them in.

Without exception those who join us were hungry and unarmed—serfs and churls from the village levies who were with Baldwin to fulfil their feudal obligations. *They apparently came in because we shouted at them to join us and they were used to following orders.*

Restormel Castle came into sight the next morning as we waded across the River Fowey. It was quite an impressive sight and Thomas and I were a little taken aback when we first saw it in the distance on the high land overlooking the river. It looked formidable and perhaps even more. Dismaying would be a better description

As a castle Restormel was just plain different—it was perfectly round perched up on a great motte of earth so the whole surrounding countryside could be seen in every direction.

There was also a fairly sizeable village next to the castle and it was right on the cart path we are travelling. No doubt that is where some of the castle's serfs and churls who we killed and captured had lived.

When we got closer we could see the castle was as strong as it looked. Around its high stone curtain wall was a moat with a drawbridge—and around the whole of it including the moat was a second great circular earth and timber curtain wall and second moat and drawbridge. Both drawbridges were raised.

"Getting us in there by force is not going to be easy. So it would be better to gull our way in, aye? So it is a task for me to handle by myself as a bishop." Thomas told me with a grin.

"You and the men stay here while I go forward with my mitre and crosier."

"What are you going to do?" I asked.

"I am a bishop am I not? So I am going to act like one by shaking my crosier at them and telling them lies.

****** *Thomas*

I was by myself as I rode slowly up to first drawbridge. "Hello the castle," I shouted towards the wall beyond the raised drawbridge. "I am Bishop Thomas. Open the gate and let me in."

Nothing happened so after a while I dismounted and took a piss. Then a couple of faces appeared on the battlements above the gate. I was still shaking my dingle when the gate opened a crack and a man in the rough clothes of a farm serf or churl slipped out and the gate quickly closed behind him.

"I am Bishop Thomas. I have news about the Earl of Cornwall. Let me in," I once again shouted across the moat.

"The Earl's dead" was the shouted rely.

"Of course he is dead. He went against Prince John did not he? And I know he is dead for sure. I buried him and said the prayers. Now open the gate and let me in. I need to talk to whoever is in charge of the castle. Is that you?"

"Of course, not. Sir Miles is the acting Constable when the Earl is not here."

"Well take me to him man. Get on with it. And get me bowl of water or ale while you are at it. I am thirsty from hurrying here to save you."

"Sir Miles is not here. He went with the Earl and his army."

"If he is with the Earl's army he is almost certainly dead. I probably buried him and said the proper prayers for him too. Who is in command here at the moment? Is it the Earl's wife?

"Not her. Alice ran off to her father this morning as soon as she heard the Earl was killed."

Then a voice hailed me from the top of timber wall next to the drawbridge.

"Who are you and what do you want?"

"I am Bishop Thomas. I am here for Prince John and I want to talk to whoever is in charge of the castle."

"That is me. Robert. I am the Constable's sergeant."

"Well drop the bridge and open the gate, Robert Constable's Sergeant. We need to talk."

"I have my orders from the Earl himself to keep it closed. I darest not. No offense to you Bishop."

"None taken. None taken. But the man who gave you those orders is dead and buried. So the orders you received from him no longer apply. I am here with Prince John's new lord for the castle, Lord William."

"That means if you do not open the gate to your new lord immediately you will be guilty of a treason most foul against our good king and his princely regent."

"Now open the gate and save yourself."

A few minutes later there were great creaking sounds and down came the drawbridge. The gate in the castle wall opened as it did. We were in without a fight.

* * * * * *

Our men were still pouring into the castle as Thomas addressed the Constable's sergeant and the small group of Baldwin's retainers who had been gathered in the castle's great hall. *Good. There are enough men here to hear his message. They will soon spread the word to the others.*

"Prince John has sent Lord William, this man right here by my side, to take the Earl's place at Restormel Castle and in the shire. I am Bishop Thomas. I am the new bishop in Cornwall and I am here representing Prince John."

What Thomas said was somewhat true, of course—he was, after all, a bishop and he was newly arrived in Cornwall; he was just not the bishop *of* Cornwall.

All the rest of it was ox shite, of course. Prince John would not know Thomas even if he leaped up and bit him in the arse.

But that was what Thomas told the wide-eyed sergeant and the castle workers including a couple of the survivors of Baldwin's attack on Trematon who somehow had already made their way back to the castle. *They must have run all the way.*

Not everyone was so easily gulled. The local priest came bustling in from the church inside the castle grounds and barely paused long enough to hesitantly kiss Thomas' ring before he started trying to ask questions. He was apparently the second or third son of a minor lord with a manor somewhere in the north and full of himself.

Ten minutes later he was in full flight back to his church to organize prayers for all those who died when the treasonous Earl attacked Edmund's poor widow.

Restormel's priest stopped asking questions when Thomas totally ignored him and proceeded to loudly explain to the little gathering that I as their new lord had been ordered by Prince John to take the head of anyone who *continued* to support the dead Earl's treasonous behaviour or questioned the Prince John's right as the King's regent to appoint a new lord.

The taking of heads did not apply, Thomas assured the dozen or so people who had assembled, to good vassals such as themselves who had loyally supported the dead Earl because he was their liege lord and would similarly pledge and honour their liege to Lord William as the new lord of Restormel.

Loyalty and adherence to tradition are important to both Prince John and to their new lord, Lord William, and would always be rewarded, Thomas explained to the assembled servants. I nodded my head in solemn agreement.

The expression on the priest's face turned to one of satisfaction when Thomas went on to assure his listeners that an exception would be made in the case of Cornwall's monks and priests because they, being men of the cloth, were *not* the late Earl's vassals.

It turned to one of horror a moment later when Thomas went on to explain that because the priests and monks were special they would not lose their heads if they were not immediately and totally loyal to Restormel's new lord; they would be burned.

I smiled and nodded as I listened to my brother. Thomas was bending the truth as a man must sometimes do. But the bending was almost certainly allowed because he was truly a proper bishop who had bought his bishopric fair and square. Besides what he was telling them was in pursuit of a good result and was somewhat true. He was, after all, a bishop.

Moreover, we had recently learned from Sir Percy that there was a bishop in Devon whose diocese had been expanded to include Cornwall. No doubt that was because Cornwall had been too poor to support its own bishop until we arrived with our galleys and coins.

If we decide to stay here, Thomas had announced as soon as we were alone, Cornwall needs to have its own bishop so we can keep out thieving priests and threaten troublesome knights and nobles with excommunication.

As a result, Thomas's threats to Restormel's constable and its priest were believable, albeit a bit premature, because we had already decided that the Company should spend whatever coins were necessary to purchase the prayers required for Thomas to serve as Cornwall's bishop and restore its diocese.

In other words, Thomas's well-meaning lies would soon be truths. Besides, Thomas was already a bishop and he was already in Cornwall so that what he told the Constable was close enough to the truth to be relied upon.

Chapter Five

We try to settle in.

Life at Restormel and Trematon regained a semblance of normalcy almost immediately because we levied no revenges or recriminations for our losses. Quite the contrary, the people of Restormel's manors quickly relaxed when they learnt Prince John and I sincerely valued their loyalty and would reward it. The old Earl's vassals, every single one of them, were not harmed for being loyal to the late Earl. So they quickly switched their allegiance to me and put Lord Baldwin out of their minds.

It may probably also helped when I made sure the word was passed that it would be instantly fatal if I ever find a slave in Cornwall or a serf not free to make his mark and become one of my vassals or join the Company of Archers. Several of Baldwin's people, it seems, had been reduced to serfs when they displeased him

What I did not tell the people living at Restormel and on its several knightly fees was that it was my intention to free all those who were slaves and serfs on the lands of Trematon and Restormel to become churls and Franklins. My brother and I had been serfs and I know what happens to them and how much they resent their masters and work against them whenever they can.

******

It was a busy time immediately after the battle at Trematon. Harold heard of our victory and immediately sent a message asking if it was now alright for his men and Sir Percy to go ashore from our boats. He also reported one of our recruiting galleys had returned from London loaded with sea-poxed apprentice archers. They are quickly recovering, he reported, and are as hungry as wolves.

Thomas and I decided he should stay at Restormel to use his priestly powers to make sure things stay calm while I rode straightaway to Trematon to get George and the boys and then ride on to Falmouth to give Harold his new orders and make sure Sir Percy had been freed.

Of course I am going to ride to Falmouth; the channel had become much too rough to take a small boat down the River Fowey and then try to row it along the coast to Falmouth; we might get blown out into the Atlantic and take weeks to get back or worse.

Before I left for Trematon and Falmouth Thomas and I made a number of significant decisions.

One was to make Restormel Castle our headquarters for the winter and perhaps permanently. It was, after all, clearly both much stronger and more defensible than Trematon and a much better location for defending Cornwall from troublesome nobles and priests. Besides, we have possession of it now and we intend to keep it even if it means more fighting.

While I am gone Thomas will draft up some parchments recognizing Trematon and Restormel and their manors as freeholds belonging to me as the new Earl. He will take them and some coins to Prince John as soon as I return. Hopefully, John will accept the coins and sign the order making me the new Earl.

Another decision that we made before I rode off to fetch George and the boys was to move our galleys and cogs from the River Fal to the River Fowey so they would be closer to Restormel. The Fowey runs close to the castle even though it is much too shallow this far upstream to get our galleys all the way up to the castle.

****** *Thomas.*

William was already off to Trematon and Falmouth by the time the Abbot and a several of the monks from the Bodmin monastery showed up at the gate requesting an audience with him.

Rufus, the Bodmin Abbot, had heard the news about Restormel having a new lord and he had come with two of his brother monks carrying a petition—they want some land Baldwin's predecessor had expropriated and "the evil Lord

Baldwin refused to return our land despite it being stolen most foul."

Abbot Rufus was absolutely astonished to find a bishop in residence when he arrived instead of the illiterate lord he expected to be able to cajole and threaten with visions of damnation and purgatory. But he quickly rallied after he invited himself to dinner and heard my diocese was in the Holy Land and in the hands of the Saracens. *I did not tell him I had only recently bought it off a far away papal nuncio after killing my predecessor and taking the coins he had intended to use to buy a position for himself in Rome.*

After his third or fourth bowl of ale Rufus began assuring his brother monks that I as a distinguished bishop of the church who had lost the lands of his diocese to the heathen Saracens surely understood the righteousness of their monastery's claim and would do the right thing by helping them convince the new lord to return their lands.

"Oh yes. I do understand, Abbot. I do indeed," I responded as I poured another bowl for myself while there was still some left. "You can count on me to speak with Lord William about your stolen lands as soon as he returns."

And when I do I will remind him monks and priests are mostly useless thieves and no mistake; they kept our mum and me and him hungry with their demands for food and coins in order for our mum to get their prayers.

******

Bodmin's monks were no more than out the door and severely disappointed when the Archdeacon of Cornwall showed up. He had come all the way from Exeter in search of a donation of lands and money "for the perpetual prayers of the church."

The archdeacon was similarly astonished to be greeted by a bishop newly arrived from the Holy Land with a ring to kiss. But he was obviously a faster thinker than the abbot; he kissed my ring and said he had heard something about the possible arrival of a bishop but had not realized I had already arrived. *He knows I am not the bishop at Exeter so he must think the diocese has been reorganized and I have been newly appointed as the Bishop of Cornwall. Hmm, there is an idea. We had already been wondering if there might be a vacancy and what it would cost to buy it with or without having to see off or kill whoever held it.*

Cornwall's Archdeacon had obviously heard that the Earl of Cornwall was going off to attack Trematon. He had arrived intending to relieve Baldwin of his sins for killing Edmund's wife and children by selling him an indulgence and accepting coins and land in exchange for perpetual prayers in the monasteries and churches of Devon and Cornwall for their souls and Baldwin's. He quickly changed his tune when I told him it was Baldwin who had died and that there was now a new and much more powerful lord at Restormel.

What I did not tell him was that the new lord was my younger brother.

Without missing a beat the Archdeacon suggested we jointly ask the new lord for a donation to the Church for the prayers needed to "consecrate" the new lord and enlist God's help in the carrying out his duties.

I responded with deep sorrow in my voice and the utmost sincerity.

"It is a pity Lord William did not know you were coming to Restormel with such a fine offer of prayers for his success. If he had known you were coming, I am sure he would have stayed here welcome you. Unfortunately I have already prayed extensively with him for his success and blessed him without getting so much as a single coin—so we will have to think of something else."

"But more prayers never hurt do they, Archdeacon, and I am sure Lord William needs them being as he is obviously neither particularly devout nor in possession of many coins. Unfortunately he has gone off to Trematon and Falmouth to attend to his more worldly affairs. Perhaps you could follow him and pray for him in Falmouth."

If the Abbot and the archdeacon ever compare the responses they received they will find they received the same reassuring answers to what I assured them was their "very reasonable" requests for a donation.

More specifically, I assured each of them I would personally recommend his very reasonable request to Lord William since I was sure both the diocese of Cornwall and my diocese in the Holy Land would get a substantial share of the resulting donations and benefits.

They had both enthusiastically agreed my suggestion of a share "for my diocese" was an absolutely splendid idea.

What they both also got in addition to my demand for a share of the proceeds, and both most reluctantly declined, was a sincere offer of transportation to the Holy Land so they could pray at the holy places where their prayers would undoubtedly do the most good.

******

It was the first time William and I have been solicited so directly for coins by high and mighty churchmen and we obviously need to learn how to better handle them. Just telling them to piss off does not sound right. Now that we are gentry we need to do it more smoothly.

Only one thing is certain—pigs will fly before either of them will get so much as a copper coin or an inch of land from either of us.

But we have got to come up with something so they go away as quickly as possible. It seems each time a churchman shows up begging for coins he expects to be fed and dined as well.

We can handle that, of course. Feeding them I mean. Talking with them when we are alone is fine because some of them are quite interesting. But what is unbearable is having a good meal ruined by having to listen to them drone on and on with religious nonsense if someone is present who might be worked for a donation.

When William returns, I am going to suggest that hereafter we ask everyone who shows up what they want as soon as they arrive and, if they are clerics, offer them passage to the Holy Land instead of money—and then regretfully announce that we are immediately leaving to "practice military training for the next crusade and the cooks are going with us because we want the crusaders to be well fed."

There is little doubt in my mind as to what will then happen; most of them will leave immediately as soon as they realize they have no prospect of either coins or free food and ale.

Alternately, if they keep pestering us we could put them on the next galley we have outbound to the Holy Land and send them on a pilgrimage whether they like it or not. They can help row.

******

The disappointed churchmen were no sooner out the door than a totally different group of men arrived—the men who run the stannaries of Cornwall, all which belong to the crown. The new arrivals consisted of three overseers of tin mines and a coiner who refines the tin and uses it to make coins. All of them were named Wartha or something like that. It was hard to tell from their speech in what seemed to be a combination of English and the unique local speech found only in this part of Cornwall.

They were not here to cadge food and coins like the churchmen; they had come because they had heard about their new lord's edict against slavery. They wanted to know if it applied to the tin mines on the Earl's lands whose revenues belong to the throne.

Their spokesman was a great bearded man with many missing teeth. *Might thought when I saw him was that he was either quite wealthy and had them pulled by a barber; or quite feisty and had them knocked out in a fight.*

"No one will work in the tin mines except slaves. Too dangerous you see. That is why we must use slaves if our good friend Wartha here is to fetch enough tin into his refinery."

What followed was a long and tedious and hard to understand explanation about how tin is mined and heated and stirred and to produce coins for the king. Listening to it made me sleepy and I had to force myself not to yawn—until something important was said.

According to them, without slaves there will be no tin ore mined or refined and without the tin there will be no coins for King Richard and Prince John. *Coins?*

"Coins? What about coins?"

"Why, tin is needed to make gold and silver coins. Hardens them up is what it does."

Only the miners had slaves and concerns about employing them; Wartha the coiner was only present to support the Warthas who operate the king's mines and refineries. His only concern was getting enough tin to mix into the coins so they would not wear out so fast.

Finally I ended the meeting by telling the increasingly shaken men that they are quite fortunate Lord William departed leaving me temporarily in charge—otherwise their heads would quite likely be on pikes at the entrance of their mines for disobeying his order to immediately free all the slaves on his lands.

"Besides," I told them, "you will get more tin and be able to coin more coins for the throne if the miners work willingly for you for pay instead of grudgingly because you are forcing them. And there is no use complaining because it was King Richard's regent, Prince John himself, who sent Lord William to Cornwall and told him to free the slaves so your production could increase.

"The same applies to your serfs. So I am going to help you since I know both King Richard and his regent, Prince John, in addition to Lord William—I am going to tell Lord William you came to assure him that you are going to free your slaves and serfs so you can produce more tin for the Crown's coins."

"Yes, there is no doubt about it. Lord William will be pleased about the slaves being freed and King Richard and Prince John will be greatly pleased when Lord William reports that you will be producing more tin so more coins can be coined."

William and I need to look into this closely. Maybe there is a way we can get some of the coins or even make some for ourselves.

Chapter Six

I am surprised.

As soon as the sun came up I started off to Trematon to get George and the boys with more than twenty of our men as an escort in case we met any reinforcements coming to assist the late and unlamented Earl. It was a brisk early morning in late September.

From Trematon we would go to Falmouth so I can meet with Harold and arrange for our galleys and cogs to move to the Fowey the next time there is favourable weather in the Channel. Martin will remain at Restormal with Thomas and continue training the men who stay here.

******

We ate a hardy breakfast in the moonlight and left at dawn because I wanted to see if a company of men could walk from here to Trematon in one day with a forced march.

It was surprisingly chilly early on but the day was beautiful and our spirits high as we walked along the footpath—until we got our feet wet crossing at the ford. The water was damn cold and it was a surprise. But we carried on and warmed up considerably as the sun rose and began to move over us on another of its endless trips around the world.

It was well past the end of the sun's passage by the time we saw Trematon in the distance. Actually it was not Trematon we saw but rather the light of the candle lantern I had a couple of our horsemen carry to Trematon yesterday so we could find it if we arrived in the dark.

Our march was somewhat of a success. A couple of men dropped out but most of them made it in time to crowd into the horse stall temporarily being used as the castle's cook house before the food ran out. The stall was being used because the castle now had more mouths to feed than its regular little cookhouse could possibly produce.

Dorothy and the men in the castle knew we were coming and they were ready. Waiting for us when we arrived were pieces of cheese, bread bowls filled with hot lamb stew with turnips and onions, and wooden bowls filled with strong ale.

I ate in the hall on the ground floor of the keep. But I was not alone. It was late and George and Lady Dorothy and her children had already eaten, but they came down the stone stairs from the sleeping room above the hall and joined me in front of the fireplace.

It was a joyful time and, unlike the men in the stable who had to share the little castle few bowls and drink from the big ladle, I had my own bowl for the ale Lady Dorothy periodically sent a servant girl scurrying off to get for me from the castle's regular cookhouse.

Two hours later Dorothy and I climbed the stairs in the dark and lay ourselves down to sleep next to the already sleeping children in one of the two beds that everyone shared. George and the other children were all huddled together on one of the sheepskin beds stuffed with straw so Dorothy and I took the other. And that was fine until we pulled the big sheepskin over us and lay side by side and tried to sleep together in the dark.

It did not work. We touched by accident and then we tentatively touched when it clearly was not an accident and then we touched and touched until she got up on her knees and I got behind her and got my dingle in her. She never said a word and neither did I.

Later that night I suffered from drinking too much ale and woke up to use the piss pot. She got up and used it herself right after I finished. Then she crawled back under the skins and in one big motion pulled my head to one her breasts and pushed it into my mouth.

After a while we began to touch each other most pleasantly until she threw her leg over me and sat herself on my dingle. Not a word was ever spoken.

******

We broke our fast the next morning quite normally. We talked of this and we talked of that and we paid attention to the children. Then it was time for me and the boys to go off to Falmouth.

The men who have been guarding Trematon would stay for a few more days and then most of them would leave and walk to Restormel—all except the dozen or so steady men we would be leaving here for the winter.

I decided to take one of the wagons in case the boys get tired from walking and needed to ride. The men will pull it just as they did to get us here. One of Lady Dorothy's men would come with us. He would ride one of the castle's two horses so we would have a messenger in hand if we needed one. I would ride the one I rode in on and the castle's second horse would remain behind.

"Be sure to send my horse back and come back yourself when you can," Lady Dorothy told me as I lifted the boys up and into the wagon."

Then she added something to make me smile and want to return.

"Every so often I need something to ride."

******

We made good time. Three days was all it took for us to reach Falmouth and start down the footpath along the river to where our boats were tied up and our men were camping.

It was a peaceful scene when we arrived late in the morning on a cool crisp day. Smoke was coming up from cooking fires and men were everywhere. There were, to my absolute amazement, even some women in the camp.

Some of the men were lounging about working on their arrows and weapons and two big groups of newly recruited men were standing out by the archery range being learned by their sergeants.

All the loungers stood up as we approached and there were friendly waves among the men as they recognized old friends. Harold quickly stood up and hurried over to welcome us and shake my hand with enthusiasm. It was a fine reception in a nice and friendly setting even though everything was still wet from last night's rain.

"Hello Hello Captain, and welcome you are and you too Master George. It is good to see all of you so safe and sound. Have you and the boys eaten, William? Would you like some bread and cheese? We have got some newly churned butter and mashed berries for the bread."

"Hello to you, Harold, and to all of you." I responded with a wave at the men. "And it is good to see you too. I have come to hear your latest news and bring you up to date on mine—and also to eat some of your bread and cheese if you have got any you can spare for us. The boys and me are always hungry. The men too."

Harold had much to tell after he shouted out an order to start cooking to someone named John who must be the cook.

Harold had obviously taken the threat seriously when word came suggesting that Baldwin might attack here instead of Trematon—as soon as we departed for Trematon he had launched the galleys and kept them anchored out on the river with all the men on board until the messenger came with word of our victory.

Now the galleys were once again moored to the river bank and he was once again training the men on shore. Even so, he told me, he always keeps a skeleton crew on every boat and has all the men sleep on the boats at night with a strong guard posted and sergeants constantly patrolling the camp to make sure the guards stay awake.

His biggest news is something he had already reported by messenger—two of our recruiting galleys returned from their trips while we were gone. Both were loaded with archers and some promising lads who thought they would like to become apprentice archers.

"Edward has got them all over to the archery range to practice. He told me yesterday he thinks some of the experienced archers might be quite useful. He said he thought Henry would be pleased when they finish being learned and get to Cyprus."

"Oh yes, I almost forgot—I released Sir Percy as soon as I got word about the fighting being over and Baldwin dead. Took him down the river to his wife in a dinghy. Done it myself actually. He is a fine old bloke, he is, and he has a lot of good stories. I gave him a gold coin for his trouble just as you said I should."

Harold's other good news was that somewhere along the coast the sergeant captaining one of the galleys found three likely young boys of George's age for Thomas's school—one was an orphan whose priest spoke highly of him and two were brothers whose mother wanted them to have a better life.

Within minutes the six boys went from shyly meeting each other to running off to the river shallows together to chase frogs.

Then I dropped my load of rocks on his head—Harold's eyes went up and his jaw dropped when I told him we would be immediately moving everything including all of our galleys and cogs and people from here to a new camp on the River Fowey because we intend to make Restormel our permanent base instead of Falmouth.

"The Fowey runs right up to Restormel does not it?" I asked him. "I know it does; I could see it from the castle wall."

"Aye, it does. Or at least I heard it does. But I doubt we will be able to get our boats too far up from the mouth of the Fowey before it gets too shallow. We will just have to find out the hard way, eh?"

Then after pausing a moment to think, he added a gentle warning.

"Well then. I better get a move on. The weather in the channel is already getting rather iffy."

Ten minutes later the sergeants were being hurriedly assembled to get the word about our move. We began to break camp almost immediately thereafter.

Chapter Seven

We move to the Fowey.

Moving our galleys and cogs and all our men to the Fowey took much longer than we expected. We got the galleys loaded and down the river to Falmouth Harbour quick enough. But when we got there the weather in the channel was not helpful and the winds were all wrong.

"We will have to wait and make a run for the mouth of the Fowey when the weather finally changes. Galleys do not do all that well in heavy weather do they?" Harold said.

About the only good thing about waiting in Falmouth for the weather to change was old Sir Percy. I had a chance to visit with him and we had a fine old time at his favourite alehouse of the two in the village. And maybe it is good thing we had to wait—while we were waiting one of our cogs came in with more recruits and hundreds of the hooded winter sheepskin clothes its sergeant captain had been sent to London to buy.

The cog's captain sergeant was one of the galley slaves we freed along with Harold when we bought them along with our first two galleys. He had been the first lieutenant on a London cog that was taken off Malta by the Tunisians. They kept him to help row instead of cutting off his head as they sometimes do. He was also named William by the way.

******

It seems that the strong winds that are keeping us here because they are blowing in the wrong direction brought the cog to us from London quite nicely despite the foul weather. Even better, its sergeant captain, William Sailor, brought good news in addition to cold weather clothes for our men—he may have found a buyer for the chests of flower paste we took off of one of our Tunisian prizes.

"I passed the word when I was outbound carrying our recruiting parties and a funny looking apothecary fellow was there waiting when I moored again at Southampton on me way back here."

"I gives him a look in the box as you told us to do and he seemed to know exactly what it was. I told him all I could do was let him look and get an offer from him for my company to consider. He said he thought some of the members of his guild might be willing to pay as much as eight hundred silver coins for every box we bring to London."

Good God almighty—the paste in those boxes is worth its weight in gold. I wonder where it comes from and how they make it?

******

Five days later the weather finally cleared and the wind changed and our galleys and cogs made a run up the coast to the mouth of the River Fowey. It was beautiful sailing weather according to Harold—and the boys and I and most of the landsmen were sea poxed and barfing over the side all the way.

We put up our sails, rowed hard, and reached the mouth of the Fowey about eight hours after the sun came up on a rainy and cloudy day in late September.   Harold's galley with the boys and I on board was one of the first of our boats to arrive.

While we were waiting at the mouth of the Fowey for the cogs and the rest of the galleys to join us, Harold and I decided to take his galley's dinghy and his strongest rowers to see how much further up the Fowey our galleys and cogs might be able to go. *Maybe we can use our galleys or their dinghies to get people and cargo all the way up to the castle.*

We loaded the six boys and a couple of shovels and axes into the dinghy to ride as its "cargo." Then Harold and I and most of the archers in his galley's crew began walking abreast of the dinghy on the footpath which runs along bank of the Fowey from its mouth at Fowey Village all the way up the river to Restormel Castle.

We were quite a crowd and rather ferocious looking with our beards and weapons. So ferocious did we look that some of the walkers coming the other way on the footpath took one look at us and ran off into the trees before we even had a chance to find out who they were. They probably thought we were Vikings returning after centuries of being away.

To our surprise Harold's sailors were able to row the dinghy quite far up the Fowey; so far, in fact, we could sometimes see Restormel Castle in the distance in front of us. According to the sailors in the dinghy the river did not become too shallow for our galleys until they reached a place about two miles downstream from the castle where the river widened and the water lost its depth as it spread out over a gravel sandbar.

We did not get the dinghy much beyond the sandbar before we reached a ford across the river and the Fowey became totally impassable even for the dinghy. We could see footprints and the cart path running from it on either side of the river and knew it was an active crossing. It was the first ford we had come across since we started up the path from Fowey Village.

Our exploring party split up at the ford—The boys and I continued upstream by walking on the footpath along the river towards Restormel; Harold and his sailors began floating and walking back downstream to our galleys.

When Harold reaches our galleys he will order them to begin rowing up the river until they reach the meadow we passed a mile or so downstream from the sand bar. It is, according to Harold, the closest we will be able to get our galleys to Restormel. It is also a good place for our galleys to be pulled ashore and shelters built for their sailors and our archer recruits even though "we may have to keep them at the castle when winter sets in."

For the foreseeable future, if we locate someplace that is even better, men and horse carts from the castle will have to travel down the path to wherever the galleys can be unloaded and then carry their cargos back up the path to the castle. A camp here for our sailors and galleys would be three miles downstream of the castle.

Harold was more than a little pleased when I agreed it was the best place to bring our galleys. He likes it because he thinks the meadow will do quite nicely for a sailors' camp and a safe place to pull our galleys out of the water. He was right; from here there is a footpath along the river all the way up to the castle. Even better, and trees in the forest next to the meadow can provide the wood we need for our cooking fires.

Unfortunately, as we soon discovered, the path along the river crosses several small streams running into the Fowey which will have to be waded to reach the castle until we can build bridges.

The cogs, of course, need more water under their hulls and cannot get upstream on the Fowey far enough to get anywhere near Restormel. They will have to either be anchored in the river much further downstream or in the estuary at the mouth of the river.

Having an acceptable place to pull our galleys ashore settled the Company's immediate future. It meant Restormel would for sure be our principal base this winter. Accordingly, the first thing that has to be done is bring our supplies and coins up the river to the castle and start building some kind of log and tent barracks for the archers and apprentices inside the castle's walls. The sailors can pull the galleys ashore and live in them until they can build permanent hovels for themselves.

* * * * * *

Thomas was absolutely thrilled when he heard a dinghy had been sighted on the river. He mounted a horse and galloped down the path along the river to meet us. He was particularly pleased to see George and meet the new boys.

"Enough for a proper school" was how he put it as he rubbed his hands in delight after giving George and me and each of the boys a big hug. It touched me to see how pleased he was to see us and the boys' warm response to him.

Everyone's mood was upbeat even though dark rain clouds were rapidly approaching and a chill wind began to blow as we walked to castle and talked along the way. Thomas' tales of the clerics and the tin miners was quite interesting. He is right that we need to know more about using tin to make coins, much more—and he was more than a little interested and echoed my own pleased and somewhat incredulous response when he heard how much the flower paste was worth.

"Why it is worth its weight in gold. Are you sure William Sailor said they would pay eight hundred for one of the little wooden cases? Could he have been mistaken and the apothecary meant eight hundred for all of the cases?"

Chapter Eight

The Company's future was being shaped.

Thomas and I sat across from each other at long table and talked in the great hall after the boys had gone off to bed. Thomas was absolutely right, and I promptly agreed, when he said the schooling of George and the boys would have to wait because he needed to go to London to carry petitions and gifts to Prince John and the papal legate. He was concerned because he feared another version of what happened to the recently departed and greatly unlamented Baldwin may have already reached them.

Our hope, of course, is that John will see us as potential allies in his battle to hold England's throne and be willing to confirm our possession of the Earl's lands and Restormel Castle as freeholds. And, of course, we most of all hope he will follow Richard's practice of selling titles and lands to raise money.

In other words, we hope to do the usual with the nobility and bribe him out of Baldwin's title and his lands. It might well work—Baldwin's wife has disappeared and we are the ones who have got possession of his castle and lands and the necessary coins.

****** *Thomas*

Early the next morning I shook William's hand, gave George a big warm and friendly hug, and left for London to see Prince John and the papal legate. I took a good two dozen of our best archers and swordsmen with me "just in case."

Taking so many archers and swordsmen with me was a necessary precaution since not only would I be carrying a chest of coins for Prince John and the papal nuncio, but I would also be taking some of the chests of flower paste to sell. London's merchants and the moneylenders who serve them are well known to be thieves when large amounts of coins and valuable cargos are at stake.

My plan was to float down the Fowey in a dinghy and take whichever galley or cog Harold suggested as being the safest for the dangerous fall waters of the channel. And that is exactly what I did. My men and I sailed for London that very afternoon in William Sailor's cog with a chest full of gold bezants and about half of the flower paste chests the apothecaries said they were willing to buy.

******

It was early November and the London air was thick with smoke when the storm tossed cog carrying me and my sea poxed men finally tied up at a wharf about a mile downstream from the bridge over the Thames. William Sailor and the cog waited at the quay whilst I hired a coach to carry me and three of my steadiest men to meet the London apothecaries.

The chests were valuable and I was taking no chances. We were all wearing chain mail under our tunics and my three guards were each carrying a sword and one of the many small rounded shields we carry on every galley. The leaves on the trees were falling; the fall season had begun and the last of the crops were being gathered in the villages.

Not to put too fine a point on it but the apothecary was absolutely astonished when I entered his shop, held out my ring to be kissed, and announced I have sixty-five chests of "the soldiers friend" flower paste in the hold of a cog tied up at Southampton available for the unbelievably low price of only eleven hundred silver coins per chest. *We are holding back fifty chests for our own use and future sales.*

"You really have that many chests? My God. Are they safe? Are they guarded?"

He immediately barred the door to his shop and sent his servant away so no one could enter to overhear or bother us while we talked. It seemed quite reasonable when he said he and his friends would need time to raise enough coins if we could agree on a price. He promised to visit them immediately and said he would know more in a few hours. Then he plied me with questions as to how we got our hands on the paste and where the cog was moored.

******

It was a dismal day and the cobblestones were slick in the thick smoky fog as our apothecary walked with my guards and I to a nearby inn where I took two rooms for the night—one for me and one for my men.

I was hungry and I had time so I ordered some chops and ale from the inn keeper and settled in to wait for the apothecary to return. *I was, to my surprise, ravenously hungry and thirsty after so much barfing at sea.*

But then I got to worrying. Somehow I did not trust the apothecary. He had asked too many questions about the chests and their location. So after I finish eating and pissing I hired a two-wheel horse cart and sent one of my men in it to tell William Sailor to beware of an attack by armed robbers and to anchor away from the wharf.

"And do not let your men separate themselves from their weapons or go ashore except two or three at a time in the dinghy."

In the morning I woke up scratching after a nice sleep and a lot of bug bites in a bed I shared with a couple of Yorkshire merchants. Everything was fine until I stood up and banged my head on a low ceiling beam. And then a delegation of four men from the apothecaries' guild showed up and tried to negotiate a lower price whilst I was still feeling poorly from last night's ale.

"I am sorry," I finally explained over my shoulder to the anxious apothecaries as I pissed in the alley next to the inn.

"Lord William authorized me to sell for no less than nine hundred silver coins per chest. I cannot sell them for a single copper less."

They grudgingly agreed—and then a second problem arose. They did not trust me any more than I trusted them. We were both afraid of being cheated or robbed.

You would think they would believe a bishop, eh? But they did not—they probably had too many dealings with them.

Finally we agreed on how to proceed—the members of the guild would come to the wharf with horse carts, and then come aboard one at a time with their coins. When each man left with his chest or chests the next man would come aboard and repeat the process. I accepted the plan because it sounded safe and I somehow knew that they really wanted to buy the chests.

******

We met on the quay the next morning. A long line of horse carts arrived with apothecaries and their coins just as our galley was tying up to the wharf with our chests of paste. Many of the apothecaries were accompanied by rough looking guards carrying clubs and swords.

The exchange process took several hours and turned out to have more value than just the coins we received—it gave me a chance to talk with the apothecaries who are waiting for their turn to buy chests.

They turned out to be somewhat of a learned group and, as a result, they had useful information about their upper class customers and the King's tax collectors—very useful information indeed.

It seems that both the absent King Richard and his regent, Prince John, who is on the throne in his absence, his young and landless brother Prince John, are operating kingly courts—and each is claiming precedence over the other in terms of receiving the King's revenues.

Richard's court is run by the man who is his chancellor and is supposed to be ruling in his absence, William Longchamp. Longchamp and his men, I was told, have been trying to raise money to pay Richard's ransom.

John and his men, on the other hand, are trying to prevent Longchamp from ransoming Richard so they can continue in power.

It is hard to believe but one of the apothecaries told me the opportunity to enrich one's self as the chancellor of the realm is such that Longchamp paid three thousand pounds of silver for the right to be Richard's chancellor and represent his interests while he was away on his crusade.

Who really was in control of the kingdom was all quite confusing and no one was more confused than the head of the apothecaries' guild. He had received a demand from both of the courts and did not know what to do.

Last week the apothecaries' guild received a demand for the immediate payment of five years of taxes from Chancellor Longchamp to help fund Richard's ransom—and then it received a visit a few days later from the Keeper of Prince John's Wardrobe warning them not to pay it because "Richard is almost certainly dead so that the coins belong to his heir, Prince John—and the Prince wants them paid directly to him." *A Keeper of his Wardrobe?*

"What pray tell," I asked, "is a Keeper and what does he have to do with Prince John's Wardrobe?"

What the guild master told me was quite interesting. Apparently the wardrobe of a king or prince is where he stores the coins he receives from his tax and scutage collections and the rents from his lands. It lets him fund his wars and diplomatic initiatives without having to go to Parliament and ask for permission or new taxes.

Accordingly, the men who gather up the taxes, scutages, and rents, and guard the wardrobe where they are stored are the "Keepers of the Wardrobe." Being a keeper is a very lucrative position as you might imagine because so many treasures and coins pass through their hands.

What I also learned is that Prince John and the keepers of his wardrobe are embroiled in a great argument with Richard's chancellor. It seems Prince John's wardrobe keepers are constantly taking the taxes and revenues being collected in the name of the king. Richard's chancellor, as you might imagine, is not happy—he says the taxes and revenues belong to the king and should be going into the king's wardrobe, the one he controls, so that he can use them to ransom the king.

******

The exchange of coins for our chests of flower paste went well. And any thought the apothecaries might have entertained about sending thieves or using their guards to seize the chests evaporated when the cog returned to the wharf and they saw all the armed men on its deck.

It took several hours but we finally finished and the coins were safely stowed away in the cog's hold. Then I hailed a horse cart for a ride through London's smoky and foul smelling streets to Prince John's court. It was in one of the castle-like strongholds *inside* the London city walls.

When I got there I pissed once again against the side of the building, gave the lice on my balls a good scratch, and then spent almost an hour talking to the Head Keeper of Prince John's "wardrobe."

His name was Blunt, the Keeper said, Sir Wilfred Blunt, and he was mightily impressed to know Lord William had supported Prince John and prevented one of Richard's supporters from stealing a poor widow's castle so he could sell it to raise ransom money. Sir William was even more impressed when I explained the financial benefits to himself and to Prince John if William was able to keep the castle as a freehold and was recognized as the Earl of Cornwall such that he replaced the greatly unlamented late Earl.

How did I get in to see John's keeper? All it took was having my archers help me push my way through the crowd of petitioners at the door and slipping a pouch of silver and copper coins (*mostly coppers with a couple of silvers on top*) to one of John's minor "wardrobe keepers" who was keeping the petitioners out. He bowed me in.

I did what I did because the apothecaries told me that Prince John's "wardrobe" is like that of Richard's and our previous kings. It contains his clothes, armour, and all his treasures. He keeps everything of value in it so it is not under the control of Parliament but rather under the control of the "keepers" of his wardrobe.

He keeps his coins in a wardrobe. Why is that? I had never heard of such a thing.

Initially the Head Keeper of Prince John's Wardrobe, his name was Sir Wilfrid Blunt and his teeth must be rotting his breath is so foul, was quite suspicious. He calmed down a bit and became much more friendly when I explained how Richard's supporter, the late Earl of Cornwall, tried to evict Lord Edmund's widow from Edmund's manor so he could sell it to raise money for Richard's ransom.

Sir William blossomed like a flower and smiled when I told him Lord William was a staunch supporter of Prince John and killed the treasonous Earl to save the widow he was attacking and help prevent King Richard's ransom from being paid.

Baldwin was a damn fool; if he had not been so belligerent we might well have bought Trematon from him for Edmund's widow instead of killing him and ending up with Restormel as well.

Sir Wilfrid liked my explanation but he was still suspicious. Why, he wanted to know, was Lord William so opposed to Richard and so in favour of Prince John?

Well, of course, I could not tell him we never had a chance to buy Trematon or we probably would have done, could I? Instead I explained about the surrender of Acre when William was there as one of Richard's crusaders and so was I there as one of the Company's priests. *In addition to being a very good archer even if I do say so myself.*

Richard killing heathen Saracens did not bother Lord William one whit I assured Sir Wilfrid; Richard breaking his word and slaughtering them after he promised he would let them go if they surrendered bothered Lord William considerably.

"Because it would make it harder for us to win back Jerusalem if the Saracens feel they could not safely surrender the city to honourable gentlemen such as your good self and Lord William."

At that point Sir Wilfrid began giving me a sales pitch as strong as some I had heard from the horse traders in the London markets—telling me that King Richard was probably dead and that it was the French who were promoting the so-called ransom so Prince John will not have money to pay mercenaries to fight them. And other ox shite things like that.

I, of course, assured Sir Wilfrid he was exactly right, and that those were exactly the reasons why Lord William greatly supported Prince John's efforts to remain in control of the English throne and become its king when Richard goes to heaven. *Hell most likely, but who knows or cares?*

"Prince John has to remain in control of England, as you know, Sir Wilfred, so he can raise money to fight the horrible French to regain the lands Richard abandoned." *Of course Sir Wilfrid knows those things. He just told them to me himself a few seconds ago.*

Then I pulled him into my pot like a fish from a black moat. I did so by assuring Sir Wilfrid of "Captain William's dedication to Prince John." I said I knew William and his men would be honoured to join John's army and follow him against Richard's supporters and to France in a heartbeat.

What I did *not* mention, as you might well imagine, was that the Company's men were never going to be available because our plan is for the Company's newly recruited fighting men to be sent off to the Holy Land to earn coins by carrying wealthy Christian and Jewish refugees to safety and transporting merchants and cargos between the ports the Company serves. Only those needed to defend Cornwall will be left behind.

"Indeed it is so Captain William can do more to help Prince John that has caused me to come to you, Sir Wilfrid."

I went on to explain how William and his men came into possession of a couple of very minor castles in distant Cornwall and needed to keep them so as to have a place to train his Company's archers before they go to the Holy Land in response to our dear Pope's latest call for Christian soldiers to fight to regain Jerusalem. *What I meant, of course, was that others will fight the Saracens and we will carry the refugees and cargos, and even the crusaders themselves if they pay in advance.*

"Honouring his word to protect Edmund's widow and having such keeps and their useless lands for training purposes and using them to help maintain Prince John in control of England are all very important to Captain William. They are so important that Captain William would deem it an honour to contribute all the coins he and his men have to Prince John for the right to hold them, and cover your expenses as well, of course."

"All it requires," I assured Sir Wilfrid, "is that Trematon and Restormel permanently remain in William's hands as the Earl of poor and useless Cornwall. Say sixty pounds for the castles and ten for your trouble?"

"Sixty is fine for the crown but I will need at least sixteen for myself," Sir Wilfrid explained to me most earnestly, "for the priests who will join me in praying for Earl William's success."

Sir Wilfrid's eyes lit up when I nodded and we began to negotiate in a manner befitting the gentleman he is. We quickly spit on our hands and shook for seventy pounds of silver for Prince John and twelve for Sir Wilfrid to help cover the huge expenses of his office and pay for a proper amount of prayers for William's success.

Everything was agreed quite quickly and Sir Wilfrid was quite pleased I had already prepared the necessary parchments. Because it was for such a good cause he said he would drop everything and have Prince John sign and seal the documents this very evening. We agreed to meet here again the first thing in the morning so he and his men can accompany me to my galley to fetch the coins.

And because Sir Wilfrid is a great gentleman, and did not become one by being slow to seize an opportunity, the first thing I did was send one of my men rushing back to London in a hired carriage to make sure the cog is anchored away from the wharf and the men remain armed and on high alert.

Sir Wilfrid's willingness to quickly sell Restormel, Trematon, and the Earldom to William was explained by what I learned the next afternoon from a talkative old law reader in the alehouse where I was celebrating my purchases and waiting for the pope's legate to return from Windsor.

It seems the father of the Baldwin's wife wasted no time in marrying her off again. He has found the poor widow a new husband, Henry FitzCount of Launceston Castle on the border between Cornwall and Devon—and he is in London on the same mission as mine. Worse, damnit, FitzCount has been similarly successful in buying Restormel and its lands by going to King Richard's chancellor, William Longchamp.

I did not have time to find out what FitzCount offered Longchamp and it really did not matter. The reality is that there were now two men claiming to be the Earl of Cornwall—and we have got Restormel and Trematon and he has Launceston.

Oh shite. William will be pissed. Now we will either have to kill yet another bastardly lord or leave more men in Cornwall in case there is a war.

Although I would have dearly liked to stay for another drink and more conversation, I did not have time to find out more from the talkative law man. So I bought the good man another round and took myself off to visit the papal nuncio, the Pope's ambassador to England, to discuss the importance of having a bishop in Cornwall who understands the importance of collecting money for the nuncio to send to the Pope.

Maybe my new friend still be here when I return; I certainly hope so. He has a purse full of news and information even if, probably because he is a lawyer, he only pretends he has no coins in it.

******

The papal legate was a seedy young Italian fellow with greedy eyes and a command of Latin even worse than mine. He listened to my tale with growing interest. And he quickly agreed with my lament about the poor bishop currently responsible for both Cornwall and Devon who is far away in Exeter and never can visit Cornwall because he is so overworked. The result, I strongly suggested, is a church which is leaving a lot of Cornish coins uncollected instead of sending them to Rome.

At least that was my story and I stuck quite firmly to it as we talked about the possibilities—in addition, of course, to offering a few coins to help cover the good man's expenses and a promise of a much larger pouch of coins if the church in Cornwall could be strengthened by the appointment of a new bishop.

Giving up my current diocese in Syria to become the Bishop of Cornwall, I modestly admitted as I handed the papal nuncio the initial coins for his expenses, was a responsibility I was ready to take on for the good of the Church and our beloved Holy Father. When I handed him the initial coins I also handed him the appointment documents I had drafted in the hope he would be able to get them signed and sealed.

Chapter Nine

Days of peace and training.

While Thomas was gone to London we began seriously training both our veteran archers and our apprentice archers on to how to fight with our new bladed pikes. It was something we needed to do—the Earl could have scattered us and won if he had come in behind us and attacked with a small group of either armoured knights on horseback or a highly organized group of men fighting the way Thomas says the Romans used to fight.

Indeed that is what we are trying to teach our men, to fight as a group instead of individually; so they support each other and such like.

What was really difficult was teaching the men to march in step so they can stay close together and we can move them around in close packed groups the way Thomas says the Romans did. It was slow going because our men were just as likely to start out on one foot as the other.

We spent hours every day practicing and it did not take long before the men started to get the hang of it. Some of the archers were becoming very good shots even when they were walking in step with their fellows. One of our earliest new recruits, the former galley slave named Henry was very useful. I immediately promoted him to sergeant and named him as my lieutenant in charge of helping me train our men.

A parchment arrived from Yoram on Cyprus whilst I was waiting for Thomas to return. It came not on one of our boats but on a Bristol cog from Cyprus carrying spices and refugees.

The cog's captain refused to hand it over until Harold gave him the silver coins Yoram had promised we would put in his hand as soon as he arrived to deliver it. It was a high price for a small cargo but Harold paid it—and then got to worrying that he might have done the wrong thing. So he sent the parchment to me by galloper and offered to come himself in case he needed to explain his decision to pay so much.

Harold did not have to come. He had made a good decision and I immediately sent back the galloper with a message thanking Harold for making it.

When I sent the galloper back I sent questions of my own with him—what does it mean that the letter came during the storm season? Is the storm season the time when the pirate galleys are in harbour so it is safe for boats with sails to sail in the Mediterranean? And, oh by the way, would he please ask around and find out when exactly is the storm season around Algiers?

What I did not ask him was probably the most important question of all—why were we paying others to carry such parchments instead of earning coins carrying them ourselves?

Yoram's letter was very encouraging. The six galleys we sent back to Cyprus all arrived safely and they and our other galleys have already made a number of successful trips carrying refugees from the Holy Land ports to Cyprus. Also, the second curtain wall is almost finished and he will soon be starting a third wall and expand the fletching works and smithy to keep our men and the refugees busy.

He also sent bad news. Poor Athol finally died of his wounds. His other bad news was even worse—one of our other Cyprus-based galleys has either been sunk in a storm or been taken by pirates. He suspects the latter but does not know for sure. Almost fifty of the Company's archers and sailors are missing.

That is worrisome because pirates rarely attack war galleys since they usually carry fighting men. Perhaps our captain overreached and tried to carry too many refugees or take too many prizes at the same time.

Yoram also reported the galley we left in Acre under Simon, Angelo and young Andy was doing quite well. But he was worried about Randolph in Alexandria because he has not heard from him for quite a while.

He said he is worried about Randolph because the refugees report the Moslem priests are telling their people that God wants them to kill everybody who is not a good Moslem—the way the crusaders sometimes kill non-Christians when they come across them.

******

Trouble and Thomas returned to Restormel on the same cold winter day. Thomas had no more than begun tucking into a good meal and telling me and George his news when a galloper arrived from Trematon. They are besieged by a large army and desperately need help.

Two minutes later and our men were assembling into their marching formations and horses were being saddled in response to a beating drum and atrocious bleats on some kind of metal horn we bought off a Falmouth merchant. Unfortunately no one knows how to blow the damn thing.

And yes we now have horses. Fourteen of them—some bought at the Falmouth fair; some from the peasants after they brought in their crops. Unfortunately, most them are barely usable for riding.

"Thomas, you stay here with George and the boys. I am going to leave you all of the apprentice archers in the training company and all the local men. Some of the new archers have become quite good and they are all highly motivated. It will give you a strong force in case this is a ruse to draw us away."

"I am taking Henry with me as my second and Robert will stay as your second. Do not take any chances. Bring in the men and livestock from the villages as well and keep

Restormel's gates closed and its drawbridges up at all times."

With that I sent off gallopers to scout ahead and we began a forced march towards Trematon.

******

We arrived in the middle of the morning and we were too late. The castle had fallen. We knew it for sure as soon as it came in sight and we could see the open gate and all the men loitering around it. I was on horseback with my three gallopers and my lieutenant riding with me.

"Form your lines and prepare to advance." I shouted over my shoulder. A few seconds later I began to hear the order repeated by the sergeant captains of each of our five companies of archers and pike men on foot.

It took less than a minute for us to become five companies of men marching forward and putting our feet down in step to the beat of each company's big rowing drum. It was an impressive sight. *Now let us hope it works.*

My gallopers and I were in the front of our companies as they marched forward. We could see men beginning to pour out of Trematon in response to our arrival. Some of them were carrying things—the spoils of war it would seem. A few were mounted but most were not.

We continued rapidly marching towards them and I could see the men on horseback chivvying the men on foot into a large group. Then three of them galloped over the field towards us.

"Who are you and what do you want?" one of them shouted. They were all three knights wearing armour.

We kept coming and I shouted an answer back.

"I am the Earl of Cornwall and I want you off my lands. Who are you?"

"I am Sir Stanley of St. Emlion he answered in Norman French and the men with me are my fellow knights in the service of Henry FitzCount, lord of Launceston and the rightful Earl of Cornwall."

"Have you seen the seal of Prince John, England's regent, on FitzCount's charter for Trematon and Restormel or for the Earldom—yes or no?"

There was no answer and we kept coming. So I shouted my question again as we got closer. Still no answer. Two of the three knights turned their horses and began walking them back towards their men so as to stay safely ahead of us.

The third knight remained for a moment longer and raised his arm in a signal for us to stop. He obviously wants to stop us for a parley. We did not and he finally turned away even though he kept looking back as he retreated ahead of us. He obviously wanted to talk but he had seen the bows my horsemen were carrying nocked and ready and was enough of a veteran to wisely stay out of range.

"What of Lady Dorothy and her children?" I shouted after him. "Are they alive and well?"

The look on his face told me all I need to know.

"Any knight who participates in the killing or taking of the wife or children of an English knight or noble will be excommunicated, lose all his titles and land, and be declared an outlaw. That is King Richard's law and I am sworn to uphold it," I shouted to him.

It was all ox shite, of course, but if that was not Richard's law it should be; it is certainly mine.

Sir Stanley started to say something but then he turned away and began trotting after his fellows before we reached him. They headed towards a group of mounted men waiting in front of the mass of foot soldiers assembling next to the gate in Trematon's north wall.

"Ride away quickly, far away, if you are an honourable knight and did not yourself raise your sword against the women and children; stay and die in disgrace and purgatory if you did."

That is what I shouted after him as I raised my hand to stop my men on horseback who were drawing their bows. In the distance I could see thirty or forty mounted men gathered around a standard. They were looking and pointing at us.

My gallopers and I halted our horses and waited as our companies passed by on either side of us to the beating of their drums. Twenty men wide and five deep they each were. I had brought three companies of archers on foot, three hundred men. Each of the five deeps was comprised of two pike men and three archers.

And they are in step and keeping straight lines; they look good by God.

Well of course their lines are straight; they have to be straight and walk to the beat of the marching drum or their sergeants will be demoted. And, of course, the long-handled pikes helped keep them straight.

Two men were carrying each of the long Swiss pikes in their left hand and every man was carrying two quivers of arrows even though only three of the five were carrying longbows. The pikes are straight so the men carrying them were all walking quickly in a straight line and putting their feet down at the same time to the beat of their rapidly beating marching drum. *It looks damn impressive. And it should since they have been practicing every day.*

"Archers nock while marching. Quiet in the ranks."

That was the order I shouted, and the sergeants promptly and loudly repeated, as the marching companies came abreast of me. As they did, Henry and I dismounted to join them. As I did, I readied my bow by stringing it and nocking an arrow. Our lines broke up a bit as they came to a low stone fence but reformed on the other side as soon as our men climbed over it.

FitzCount's mounted knights and their squires came at us soon after we climbed over the fence and reformed our ranks. They were initially walking their horses but obviously about to break them into a trot and then charge. A great disorganized mass of men carrying clubs and assorted weapons was walking and running behind them.

But not all were coming—several mounted men turned their horses and began trotting away to safety. And some of the walked men stopped walking forward and began to move back. They were the smart ones—they had seen us move to the beat of our marching drum and knew we were not a mob of peasants who would be easily broken.

"Ready with the Pikes"... "Halt." That was what I shouted as the knights and their squires got closer, broke into a trot, and closed their helmet visors.

I raised my right arm but waited until I was sure it was not a false charge to see our reaction. It was not and they broke into a gallop.

After a brief pause to let the charging knights get close enough so it would be too late for them to stop, I shouted the order.

"Up pikes." ... "Set pikes."

It was an impressive sight as our side by side companies halted and the pikes the first two men in the line have been carrying with their left hands were suddenly elevated and revealed for the first time.

Several of the mounted men riding towards us who had been hanging back and many in the mob walking behind them were obviously impressed when they saw our disciplined ranks and our pikes come up— they pulled up and some of them were able to turn away and save themselves.

It was too late for many of the charging knights and the men running behind them when they finally realized that we were not an ill-trained mob of hastily mobilized serfs and churls. And it was very much too late for those in front. *And, of course, once their visors came down the knights could hardly see at all. Bad luck for them.*

The company sergeants were watching my raised right arm. I dropped it, shouted "Raise your pikes, pick your man, and push." And I kept shouting it and pumping my arm up and down as soon as the knights drop their visors and begin their charge.

All along the columns the sergeants began loudly repeating the order "Raise your pikes, pick your man, and push; raise your pikes, pick your man, and push. ......"

Our men give a great cheer as a great cloud of arrows reached out towards the charging horsemen and the pikes came up—and the charging knights kept blindly coming on towards us even though some of their horses were beginning to go down and trip those coming along behind them.

So far so good. We have many more arrows.

The result was what any veteran soldier or horseman would expect. Even highly trained horses do not react well to being hit with arrows—fewer than half of the charging knights reached our pikes and none got past them. Well that is not exactly correct.

Charging horses always stop when they impale themselves on two or three long pikes set firmly in the ground. It is their riders who do not stop—they flew through the air and knocked over the men in some of our files like bowling balls on the village green.

Once the knights are down they do not get up. The knights who flew off their horses and landed in our ranks promptly had their throats cut or got stabbed into their heads through their eyes. And those on the ground in front of us did not get up either. Not after I gave the command to resume our march and our men marched past them and stabbed them as they went by.

Very few of what was left of the charging mob of men on foot behind the knights even reached our lines. Most did not. They either immediately turned and ran or they were felled by the cloud of arrows that rained down upon them both as they charged us and then after they turned and began running away in a desperate effort to escape.

Chapter Ten

I am distraught.

Discipline fell apart after the battle. Our sergeants lost control as our men spread out over their fallen foes to plunder them. I was not there to stop them. I remounted my horse and rode for the castle gate with my gallopers—and on the way used my sword to cut down a couple of FitzCount's fleeing men who were between me and the gate.

What I saw as I rode over the lowered drawbridge and through the gate were the bodies of some of the men I had left to defend the castle; what I saw when I dashed up the stairs two at a time to upper level was even worse—Dorothy and the two girls had been literally hacked to pieces.

******

Henry FitzCount was not among the dead knights. He must have held back when his men charged. To my surprise the very next day FitzCount sent two heralds. They proposed a truce and a parley.

I agreed. There is nothing to lose by talking and if I can get close enough to FitzCount I will kill the bastard truce or no.

It happened this way. The morning after the battle two knights appeared in the big field behind Trematon with a man blowing some kind of horn to announce them.

My irate response when we met was deliberately loud enough to be heard by my men in the formation behind me.

"Are you two cowardly children killers like Henry FitzCount or are you real and honourable knights?" were my first words before they could say anything.

I was goading them you see; and heating up my men while I did it.

"We are knights in the service of King Richard, Monsieur," the older one answered from about twenty paces away.

"I am Phillip of Calais and this is Louis. He is from Calais also. Henry FitzCount is our cousin."

"I do not believe you. If you were Norman knights sworn to Richard you would not be in front of me on behalf a cowardly killer of young girls, the children of a lord who fell fighting the Saracens with King Richard."

"King Richard will cut off your dingles and crucify you. That is what Richard will do when he hears you helped that cowardly scum FitzCount kill one of his lord's wife and little children."

I kept taunting the two knights without giving them a chance to speak; I wanted my men to hear what I said.

"FitzCount is such a coward that he abandoned his men and ran from the field did not he? Did you two little flowers run away with him when he abandoned his men and ran?   If so, why should I parley with cowards such as you two and the disgraceful little peasant you represent?"

The two French knights were taken back. This was not at all the reception they had expected.

"No monsieur, we are sworn to King Richard and newly arrived in England this very month."

"I will accept your word about that even though I find it hard to understand. I personally served with Richard in the Holy Land and I know he has no use for cowards who are only capable of killing children."

And then I added very slowly and pointedly, "or those who choose to ride with them."

"Sir Henry is not a coward,' interjects the younger man. He sent us here to challenge you to a "trial of arms" to let God settle the dispute between you.

"He issues a challenge to me does he? Well that is good news. Very good news even though my men will be sorely disappointed—every one of my men was taken to see the children he butchered and each and every man has sworn to kill him. I myself, and Bishop Thomas on behalf of the Holy

Father, have each offered one hundred gold coins for the coward's bollocks and dingle."

The two French knights were truly stunned as I continued. *Good. They do not realize I am speaking to my men as well as to them.*

"So Henry FitzCount challenges me eh? Well that means I name the time and the place and the weapons is that not so? And no substitutes are allowed so he cannot hide?"

"Of course, Monsieur" responded the older man.

"Good. I name tomorrow at noon right here on this very spot. Both of us on foot with no one else within two thousand paces. Is that acceptable to you and you will swear on your honour to have Henry FitzCount here to face me himself and not a substitute?

"Yes, Monsieur, that is acceptable. We swear it."

"Good. And as his seconds will you swear to denounce him to King Richard as a coward and take all your men and leave his service if he refuses to pick up his weapons and fight me here at noon?"

"Of course, Monsieur. We swear it."

"Good. I will meet him here on foot at high noon. I am English and he is English so the weapons I choose will be English—daggers and English longbows. No other weapons. Are you agreed?"

The French knights were surprised by my choice of weapons but they nodded their agreement. They had no choice. With that I turned my horse and cantered back to the castle. My men had heard every word.

Of course I chose the weapons I knew best. I am not stupid you know.

* * * * * *

We tended to the dead and wounded and camped on the field that night. At noon the next day my men were all assembled in their companies and ranks behind me. They were watching as I walked out into the empty field with a couple of longbows, four quivers of "heavies," iron-tipped arrows capable of piercing chain in case he was wearing it as I would be, and a skin of water.

Even my brother Thomas was watching. He had heard about the challenge from a galloper yesterday and damn near killed a horse to get here from Restormel.

A smaller crowd of fifty or so men was assembled and watching from some distance away on the other side of the field. Many of them were mounted so I assumed one was Henry FitzCount and rest were the surviving knights and squires of Launceston Castle and its manors and mercenaries.

After a while one of the mounted men dismounted and began walking into the field with a bow in his hand. *Hot damn the fool is coming.* I walked towards FitzCount for a while and then just stopped and waited for him come to me.

The two bows I had brought with me were both strung and I proceeded to stick some of my arrows in the ground for fast access. The rest are in the quivers on my back in case I need to move around.

FitzCount was barely out of my range when he stopped and waved his hand in the air. Suddenly five or six horsemen broke away from his crowd of supporters on the other side of the field and begin galloping towards me with their swords in their hands. A trap!

Thomas and I had been worried about such a betrayal because the knights that delivered FitzCount's challenge were French. *They have all have the pox, you know, and it affects the way they think. It is well known they get it because they eat disgusting things like toads and snails.*

I had suspected treachery. That is why I did not go all the way to the middle of the field.

My response to the charging riders was to drop my bows and run for my life as fast as my feet could move. My head was down and I was moving my legs as fast as I could when I heard a booming English voice in the distance give a command from somewhere in front of me.

"Nock your arrows and shoot as soon as the bastards are in range. Keep shooting. Rapid advance."

I did not look back but I knew I was in mortal danger when I heard the pounding hoofs rapidly closing on me from behind and the familiar noise of arrows swishing over my head. I was totally out of breath as I literally dove headfirst into the frontline ranks of our pike men. *Safe by God.*

Unknown hands pulled me to my feet even though at first I could only stand by leaning over with both hands on my knees. Only after I took a couple of deep breaths was I able to turn around and look as I continued to gasp and try to catch my breath.

Most of my would-be murderers' horses were on the ground along with four of their riders. One horse was still on its feet with its rider attempting to gallop away through the cloud of arrows coming down all around him. And then he too went down.

Closer in one of my would-be murderers was struggling to get out from under his fallen horse.

You dishonourable swine did not know about English archers and longbows did you?

My heart was pounding and I was still gasping for breath and breathing deeply when I heard a command in the distance and the sergeants around me began shouting "Cease pushing ... Cease pushing."

After a moment's pause to settle myself down, and a heartfelt thank you and acknowledging wave of my hand to the men in the ranks around me, I began walking out to the downed knights. Thomas and several of the company sergeants were close behind me and soon caught up with me.

The second closest rider was still trying to get out from under his horse as I walked up to him. "Ransom... Ransom" he began shouting anxiously as he saw me walking towards him.

I look down at him and responded with a mocking "Honour... Honour" as I leaned over and stabbed him in the eye—and pushed my dagger in as far as it would go.

My third and fourth would be knightly assassins were already dead from multiple arrow hits and broken bones. The fifth was not. He was out at the far distance of arrow range so his horse undoubtedly went down early in the first flight of arrows.

The knight's horse going down so quickly probably saved him when the archers turned their attention to those still on their horses who got closer to them. This knight, like the other three, appeared to be a Norman. He was in French armour and his leg was broken. *His armour looks to be so heavy that he probably could not get up by himself even if his leg was not broken.*

By now the white heat of my anger was gone and I was tired, very tired. Exhausted actually. So I sat myself down on the ground nearby and listened as Thomas and a couple of sergeants questioned him.

"Tell me everything." My priestly brother demanded of the French knight as he ripped off the man's helmet. "Who gave you the orders to do such a foul deed and what were you promised?"

Our captive and Thomas had an interesting conversation, a very interesting conversation. He was obviously a Norman and at first he refused to talk and babbled on about paying a ransom and pleading for mercy.

But he changed his mind after Thomas pulled him out from under the horse with a sweet smile and twisted his leg a couple of times—his broken leg.

He was, the man told us, a Norman knight recently arrived at Launceston as a mercenary and he gave us surprising information. He was in great pain and desperate to tell us everything he knew.

It took a while but we got it all. Then Thomas stopped twisting his leg and motioned for one of the sergeants to cut his dishonourable goddamn throat.

We were alone on the field by the time the questioning stopped. The mounted party at the other end of the field turned and rode away even before we finished and walked back to our men. Behind me our men were stripping the knights of their armour. They will make nice trophies if we do not sell them or melt them down to use as arrowheads on our armour-piercing heavies.

******

What the late and unlamented Norman knight had told Thomas was quite surprising—it was the Earl Baldwin's widow Alice, or "Lady Alicia" as he called her, who was responsible for all the deaths and trouble. It was Alicia who had demanded Baldwin evict her half-sister Lady Dorothy from Trematon and then attack it when the eviction failed. *Her half-sister?*

When her husband Baldwin and his brother were killed it was Lady Alicia who demanded Henry FitzCount attack Trematon and kill Dorothy and her children. If he did, she had promised, she would marry FitzCount and bring him all of Baldwin's lands. What the knight could not tell us was why she did it. *Kill her own sister and her little nieces? Her own sister and little children? That is truly disgusting.*

What was particularly surprising to me was hearing Alice and Henry FitzCount were already on their way to his Launceston Castle and betrothed to be married in the spring. They left yesterday right after we retook Trematon—before FitzCount sent the French knights as heralds with the challenge I accepted.

It was all a gull to get me out in the open so they could kill me.

Good God—Alicia or whatever her name is probably thinks I am dead and she and FitzCount will end up with the lands and revenues of both Trematon and Restormel in addition to those of Launceston. Then what? Will she kill FitzCount and use her lands to trade up again with another marriage to another lord. I do not doubt it; she is obviously as ambitious for herself as we are for George. But her own sister and her little nieces?

Chapter Eleven

Revenge.

"We have got to settle this once and for all, William. It will not wait. We are all in danger, even George, until that woman and her French lord are gone to hell where they belong."

Thomas thought we should march our men straight to Launceston Castle and keep them there until we starve FitzCount out and take it.

"Let us go starve them out kill the lot of them. We need to get it over with before they regroup and come to kill us and little George," was Thomas' opinion.

George? My God what will we tell George about Lady Dorothy's daughters? It will give him nightmares.

I told Thomas I agreed with him. And I did—both to end the risk to George and because I could not get the sight of Dorothy and her two little girls out of my mind.

******

Launceston is in Cornwall on the Devon border just before you reach the River Tamar. The Tamar is the great natural barrier, a moat if you will, where Cornwall ends and Devon begins. Cornwall is mostly important for its tin mining and refining. The mines and refineries are mostly on the fairly useless lands belonging to me as the Earl of Cornwall, but the tin and the right to mine it and refine and coin it belong to the crown.

Indeed, Thomas suddenly recalled, some of the tin miners who visited him came from Launceston. When we get there we need to look them up to find out what they know about coining and make sure their slaves and serfs have been freed. If they had listened carefully and done what they had been told, they would have employed free men and increased the number of coins they were sending to London for Richard and John to argue over.

Things moved right along and we left for Launceston almost immediately. We appointed a handful of men to remain at Trematon and clean it up, and I sent a galloper to Sir Percy in Falmouth inviting him to come to Trematon with his wife and be its permanent castellan.

Where Thomas and I were not in agreement was about Restormel. Thomas wanted to come with me to Launceston and I wanted him to return to Restormel and stay there with George until I returned.

I finally won Thomas' grudging acceptance because my argument was better—George and the boys needed him at Restormel for their learning and protection; and I needed him there to organize the supplies and reinforcements I would need if I was to take Launceston and the heads of the French vipers who infested it.

We both agreed we should try to take Launceston before it was time for our galleys to sail for the Holy Land in the spring; what we did not discuss is what we would do if we do not take Launceston before the newly planted crops began to spring up and it was time for the galleys to sail.

******

Two days later our men finished burying the dead and we started for Launceston. Just before we left Sir Percy galloped in from Falmouth to take over Trematon. He was more than a little pleased with his new appointment.

"I am honoured and the wife will be pleased. Finally got herself a proper castle to fuss over. She will be over the moon with joy."

******

It took us almost a week to get to Launceston. It took so much time because the leaves had long ago fallen from the trees such that we had to stop at Restormel to get the tents and supplies and weapons we would need for a winter campaign.

When we finally got to Launceston we found the castle's drawbridges up and its battlements manned. FitzCount obviously expected us. Some of the men who watched the failure of his attempt to murder me would have had more than enough time to get here and warn him before we could arrive and begin our siege.

One look at the castle and I knew there was no way I was going to throw our men's lives attempting an attack it. It was far too strong. We would have to encircle it and starve the bastards out with a siege.

Two cold and boring weeks later and a surprise messenger arrives—my brother Thomas and he was accompanied by Bishop Pierre of the diocese of Cornwall and Devon. *And Thomas quickly took me aside and told me he did not think the Bishop knew he had been to London to see the papal legate about splitting off Cornwall as a separate diocese with Thomas as its bishop.*

The Bishop's story unfolded in front of the fire in Launceston Village's only alehouse. He had heard, he told us, about the Earl's intention to attack Trematon and had been on his way there in an effort to try to stop the attack.

With a great heaving sigh of painful lament the good man explained that his mule went lame and, because he has painful bunions that make it difficult for him to walk, he had only gotten as far as Restormel when he learned he was too late to save Lord Robert's family.

It was at Restormel where he had first heard about me bringing my men to Launceston and my quite understandable intention to put Launceston under siege and take vengeance on Lord FitzCount. He had come here with Bishop Thomas, he said, to once again offer his services as an honest broker in the cause of peace.

It was a heart warming story except for the not so minor fact that all the while the good Bishop is telling his tale to me Thomas was standing behind him shaking his head negatively.

In a nutshell, or so he said, Bishop Pierre proposed to approach Lord Henry and his betrothed in the castle to see if he can work out some kind of compensation of land and money for the spilled blood and the wrongs that my men and I have suffered.

"And, of course, something for Lady Dorothy's family as well."

"It sounds like a wonderful idea and a good man you are for being willing to make the effort."

That was how I responded to him after I saw my brother standing behind him and emphatically nodding his head that I should agree.

******

"He is lying through his teeth" were Thomas' first words as soon as we were alone. "They must have gotten word to him somehow. How else could he have known FitzCount and the viper are here or known about what happened at Trematon?"

"The papal nuncio told me the bishop is FitzCount's cousin when we talked about Cornwall's gentry and who might oppose the establishment of a new and separate diocese for Cornwall. I do not think he knows we are brothers and close; he thinks I am an unemployed bishop who had to flee the Holy Land and is teaching your children and others in exchange for my food and a place to lay my head."

The next morning Bishop Pierre of Cornwall and Devon walked up to the Launceston drawbridge, and into the castle. It had been lowered and then quickly raised behind him as soon as he crossed it.

"Praise God," the Bishop of Cornwall and Devon shouted to us as he came back over the drawbridge beaming several hours later.

He had good news. FitzCount was willing to make amends with a considerable, a very considerable, amount of money and land so "bygones will be bygones."

I did not even know Launceston had so much land.

Moreover, the good bishop had taken it upon himself to arrange a meeting between FitzCount and me to finalize matters and make our marks on an agreement and arrange the payments associated with it.

If I agreed with the terms, the bishop said, we would all meet in the tiny Launceston religious chapel where pilgrims stop to pray on the road to Devon. It was the tiny wood and stone building that stood near the dirt track that runs along the edge of the village and continues on to the castle.

To enhance and guarantee everyone's safety, and to insure the Church will accept and bless the agreement, each of us will be accompanied by only one man, a bishop—he and Thomas.

And, oh yes, I will, of course, have to temporarily pull my men back out of the village so Sir Henry feels safe to walk alone down the track and enter the pilgrims' chapel.

Chapter Twelve

Betrayal and a great surprise.

Henry FitzCount's offer of a substantial number coins and a large tract of land in exchange for a permanent peace was actually incredibly generous, and almost certainly too good to be true. As a result, Thomas and I and the good bishop of Devon and Cornwall eagerly awaited FitzCount's arrival the next morning.

We were not disappointed. After Thomas and Bishop Pierre walked through the village to make sure it was empty of my men, Bishop Pierre took a piece of linen out from under his robe and waved it at the castle. Moments later the castle gate opened and Fitzcount walked briskly over the drawbridge and then waited at the end of it while the two bishops used the side door to the priest's dressing room to enter the chapel to make sure it was also empty. It was.

FitzCount and Bishop Pierre entered the chapel first as we had previously agreed. Then Thomas and I followed them into the tiny church. We too entered by walking through the tiny side door into the very small room where the priest puts on his robes before entering the chapel to conduct a service.

By the light coming in through the opening high on the walls of the chapel we could see FitzCount and the good Bishop standing on its dirt floor. The chapel itself was a tiny little thing with its little wooden altar against the wall and space for no more than twenty or so people to pray—there was obviously no one in the building except the four of us.

FitzCount and his cousin motioned us to shut the door to the priest's dressing room and come in. They had already, as we had agreed, barred the front door to the outside so no one else could get in.

What FitzCount was offering in compensation was so large we had decided to accept it and kill him later—except we fully expected some kind of trickery and betrayal. We just do not know what form it would take or when it would occur.

We soon found out. I was reading the agreement and nodding my agreement to its generous terms when the door to the little dressing room opens—the door I shut behind me a few minutes ago, and three men crowded into the little chapel carrying the long broad swords favoured by Norman knights. They were not in armour and had mud and dirt on their jerkins.

Where the hell did they come from?

FitzCount snickered and said "You are both under arrest" in French as his men reached out to take each of us by the arm. They were confident, smiling broadly, and holding swords at their sides whereas we are obviously unarmed and outnumbered.

"Are you sure you are doing the right thing?" I asked FitzCount rather benignly.

"Oh yes. Restormel is now mine and Edmund's castle too." And then with a bit of arrogance and a big smile he added "and your heads are mine too."

"And you Bishop Pierre. Do you agree with his lordship?"

"Yes I do. God wills it."

"We have heard those words before, have not we Thomas?"

"Yes we have. Indeed we have." Thomas agreed with an understandably sad sound to his voice.

Then he looked at me in the faintly lit little room and did what I expected him to do; he blinked a heavy blink with both eyes and we both silently counted to three as we had practiced and done together so many times in the past.

Our hands came out from under our baggy tunics with the knives in each hand that each of us always has strapped to his wrists.

Thomas got his man very cleanly but I was a split second late and partially missed the Norman holding on to my right arm—he jerked back instinctively as he raised his sword and tried to bring it around so I only succeeded in slicing him across his cheek and across his eye.

My man screamed and reached for his eye instead of swinging his sword around and coming at me with it. It was a bad mistake.

I got him in the throat with a thrust from the knife in my other hand and finished it by shoving my first knife high into his stomach and pushing downward.

He looked at me in stunned surprise and let out a big fart and a groaning scream as he staggered backwards a half step to the wall and slowly began to slide down it. I help him along by pushing downward with the knife I had stuck in his belly.

Thomas was already cutting into the throat of the third man with his other knife when I leaned over and sliced into his throat with the knife in my other hand to help finish him off—and came close to cutting Thomas's hand when I did.

It was over in the blink of an eye and the would-be Earl and his bishop cousin were as surprised and unprepared as their men who were still choking on the floor and making the usual sounds of distress from dying men.

The bishop and FitzCount just stood there and watched with their mouths open in the split second it took us to cut down their men.

Then the bishop squealed like a pig as I stepped forward and jerked the knife out of the third man's throat—and put it at his stomach and slowly and deliberately pushed it in all the way to its hilt while I held the bishop's robe so he could not back away.

"I wish we had more time to talk," I said with a snarl over the bishop's high pitched squeals.

"I would like to know more about why you think God wills the stealing of the homes of widows and the murdering of innocent children."

FitzCount suddenly came out of his trance when he heard me speak. He knocked the little altar over as he tried to scramble away backwards. He got almost to the door to the Priest's little dressing room before I reached him and knocked him down, and then pulled open his robe and grabbed him with one hand and used the knife in the other—to cut off his balls and dingus so he would bleed to death.

I leaned down whispered a message to him after I finished.

"It might help the pain if you were to pray for the souls of Lady Dorothy and her daughters."

It took FitzCount quite a while to roll around on the chapel's dirt floor and die, and he sobbed and screamed all the way out.

Chapter Thirteen

Unexpected outcomes.

Thomas and I explored the tiny priest's dressing room while FitzCount was finishing his dying.

It took a while but we finally found it—the wooden wall with the pegs to hold the priest's vestments swings out as a door. There was narrow tunnel behind it with a candle still burning in a boat's lantern.

"I will go get some of our men," Thomas said.

"Best you go out the front door and keep the chapel between you and the castle so they cannot see you from the walls," I suggested.

Twenty minutes later three brave volunteers, *or ambitious men seeking the recognition they will get*, were silently leading us very slowly down a long narrow tunnel.

I was the fourth man in the line. Each of the three men walking in front of me was carrying a candle lantern Thomas and a dozen or more of our men were behind me clutching their bows and short swords.

The tunnel was obviously some kind of mine shaft; it was damp and cold and oppressive, but not draughty. My initial impression was that it was quite old and no longer in use except as a secret passage out of the castle.

We were walking and stumbling along very slowly and cautiously behind the candles in the semi-dark. Except for the candle holders and me, each man's hand was holding tightly on to the hooded coat of the man in front of him; his other hand was inevitably holding a sword or bow and trying to use it to touch the ceiling at the same time so as to not knock his head.

Our three men in the very front walked very slowly and carefully carrying the candle lanterns. Everyone else was shuffling along behind them in the darkness and periodically scrapping along the side of the tunnel to skin his knuckles or bang his head. No order was ever given, but every man instinctively knew not to say a word even when he banged his head or skinned his knuckles.

It was a slow journey and we seemed to be walking downhill for quite a while. But maybe not; it was hard to tell. Then the tunnel changed and we began going mostly uphill with a stone step or two every so often. And each of the stone steps inevitably stubbed the toes of each of the men behind me as they reached it.

Our slow and cautious walking ended at a wooden door.

******

The lantern carriers stopped when they reached the door. The man at the very front immediately turned and made a questioning gesture with his hands to ask me what I wanted him to do. As I looked around the three men standing in front of me I could vaguely see the outline of a wooden door in the flickering candle light.

I nodded and waved my agreement to proceed, and then held both my breath and my sword as the first lantern carrier pulled on the door and it opened a crack with his sword at the ready. It creaked loudly.

After a long and cautious wait nothing happened. So he slowly opened the door all the way and we started forward once again. After we had walked a while we reached a widened passageway, almost a cavern, and began walking up a slope past what look like old mining tools and large rocks which have been pushed aside so people could pass.

We came around a bend in the passage and almost immediately came to another wooden door.

Once again our brave lamp carrier leading the way slowly cracked it open and peered inside. Finally, with the door squeaking loud enough to wake the dead, he pushed it all the way open and we entered. Once again our line began moving slowly forward as we cautiously followed him. I do not know about the others but I could hear my heart pounding.

I smelled the piss before I got past the second door. I have smelled cat piss like this many times before and I know exactly what it was we were entering—it was a store room for the castle's food supplies and it had cats in it to keep away the mice and rats. The cats piss and shit on the floor below the barrels and sacks of food; that was what I was smelling.

Our lantern carrier stopped and held his lantern high so we could see around the room. What we could dimly see in the flickering light was a cavern filled with sacks and amphorae of grain and tubs and barrels of what must be butter and cheese. There were big piles of turnips and onions stacked on wooden planks.

Everything was sitting on planks held up by logs to keep them off the damp ground. Keeping everything off the ground in such a way was also important because it allowed the castle's cats to get at any hungry mice and rats that might be prowling around underneath them looking for a meal. There were even deer carcasses hanging from hooks in the wall. We were in the castle's larder.

"Keep holding the lanterns up high" I ordered their carriers in a whisper as more and more of my men slowly shuffled into the room. Everyone was extremely tense and excited including me.

No one said a word. Then I had an idea and whispered an order into a number of ears as I gently pushed some of the men past the lamp carriers and towards the entrance door at the far end of the larder.

"Go forward slowly and help guard the entrance to the larder. Do not let anyone in. Be totally silent."

As I whispered the order I gently pushed the men past the lamp carrier towards the entrance at the other end of the cavernous room. *I had an idea.*

I began whispering new orders when all the men were finally out of the tunnel and into the storeroom and four or five of them we in place to hold the entrance door.

"Everyone pick up a sack of grain and carry it down the tunnel to the pilgrim's prayer house where we first entered. Stack it up inside little church. Then wait there; do not go outside and show yourself. Piss or shite in there if you have to go."

For what seemed like forever our men carried food out of the castle's larder. Periodically I stopped the carrying so the men in the little prayer house could return through the narrow tunnel to get another load.

Then it happened. Someone in the castle came to get food from the storeroom. The door opened, and a terrified woman screamed and dropped the candle she was carrying.

And at the same time, goddamnit, the sudden draft of air coming through the open door caused our candles to flicker and go out—and everyone started talking at once.

"Silence goddamnit. Silence." …. "No talking; defend the door. Do not let anyone in," I shouted in the darkness to the guards near the storeroom entrance.

"We are going to keep carrying the food out. Feel around for it. And get the damn hinds off the hooks if you cannot find any more sacks of grain or cheeses to carry."

"And does anyone have a set of flame rocks they can spark to light the candles?"

No one did. We had to work by feeling and touching in the pitch blackness.

******

We were soon not alone. The alarm had been sounded and an unknown number of Launceston's defenders rushed to the scene—and then backed away instead of attacking us. Probably because no one likes fighting in the dark. It was a standoff we were winning because we were continuing to stumble around and remove the castle's food reserves.

Finally a voice in the distance called out in Norman French. "Who are you?"

"Henry FitzCount and his bishop have run away and abandoned you," I shouted. "And now your food is gone. So it is time to save yourselves and Lady Alice. We will not stand in your way if you leave peacefully."

I was telling a lie. Of course we would not stand in their way. Since they are totally dishonourable knights we are going to repay them in kind by having our archers stand to one side and shoot them down as they ride past us.

After a long pause there was a question.

"How do we know we can trust you, Monsieur?"

"You cannot. But we let the Bishop and Lord FitzCount go free after our parlay so you can trust me when I swear on my oath as a knight that we will give you, their followers, the very same courtesies and freedom that we gave them." *That is for damn sure.*

"in about an hour you will be able to see we have pulled back from the entrance to the castle drawbridge and there are boats at the river crossing. And you can leave the castle servants without losing your honour—Lord William will retain them in their positions if they pledge their liege to him."

Not that you care about honour or have any left to lose.

They obviously did not believe me. As a result, our standoff continued for over an hour until what is left of the food was on its way down the tunnel. At that point there was no need for us to fight our way into the castle and lose men; so we turned around followed the last of the castle's food stores as they were taken into the tunnel and carried away to the chapel.

I was pulling everyone back because I wanted the knights to come in and see their food is gone—and I want to organize the archers to give the knights the warm welcome they deserve when they make their sortie and try to escape, as they almost certainly will as soon as they find out that we have carried away most of their food.

******

Within an hour we were out of the tunnel and our archers were off to the side of the castle gate in five deep formations with our pike men in the first two ranks as usual. We waited all the rest of the day and early evening—and nothing happened. Could they have escaped through another tunnel? It was certainly possible. According to the villagers the whole area is honeycombed with old mines and tunnels.

Thomas and I finally dismissed the men long after the sun went down and the night got colder. We were billeting them in the villagers' low ceiling hovels and they were told to sleep with their clothes and sandals on and their weapons at hand.

Thomas and I were exhausted and asleep in the smoke-filled hovel nearest the little pilgrim's chapel where we killed Henry FitzCount and his men. The little chapel now had some of our men guarding its tunnel. We could not use it as a shelter because it was now stuffed from its floor to its low ceiling with sacks and barrels of foodstuffs from the castle.

The villager and his family were gone from the hovel where Thomas and I were sleeping shoulder to shoulder with almost two dozen or more of our men. It was so crowded that most of us had to sleep sitting up. But the heat of our bodies warmed the place and we were content as we shivered and tried to sleep.

Chapter Fourteen

We take our revenge.

Dawn was still two hours away when both of the castle's gates suddenly opened and Launceston Castle's two drawbridges began to come down almost simultaneously. Visibility barely exists because of the cloud cover and waning moon. It was, I later admitted to Thomas, the best time for a sortie and I should have seen it coming.

Our men poured out of the village when the French sortie began and the cries of warning and alarm began to sound. Most of our men were not even close to their company's position when the mounted Norman knights began pouring out of the castle and over the drawbridge to where we were no longer waiting in force because of the cold.

Some of our men were able to reach their places and begin closing up to create the compact formations as we have so often practiced. Most of them, however, were not ready. They were either lost in the cold darkness or were still coming from the hovels where they had been sheltering from the cold.

Thomas and I dashed out the door and arrived at the nearest company just as the horses ridden by the first French knights begin clattering across the drawbridge. A quick thinking sergeant was already bellowing out orders to the archers and pike carriers. *And he was impressing me by making the decisions I should have been making. I must remember to get his name.*

"Launch at the near drawbridge and keep shooting. Launch at the near drawbridge and keep shooting. Shoot... Shoot. Goddamnit... Up pikes... Up pikes. Pike men crouch down." *Are they coming to fight?*

Within seconds everything became clear. FitzCount's knights and their men on foot were trying to escape from Launceston rather than coming out to fight us.

Thomas and I and everyone around us were launching arrows as fast as we could push them out—until we emptied our quivers. We could hear the clattering hoofs and see the vague outlines of the horsemen, but we could not see specific targets. It was all we could do because it was too dark to see.

"Do you think we can stop them?" my priestly brother gasped as he grabbed his last arrow from his big quiver and shot again.

"Cannot tell. We will know soon." I gasped back as I launched one of mine right behind his. *It was a hard run to get here and we were both still out of breath and freezing cold.*

What Thomas was asking about was what we did right after it got dark last night—we scattered two wagon loads of caltrops right where the French knight's horses would be stepping as they come off Launceston Castle's outer drawbridge.

We were using every one of the rusty old caltrops we bought from the Hospitallers' Acre fortress. We had brought them with us when we came to Launceston.

Well of course we brought them to Launceston; we are not exactly virgins when it comes to besieging a castle are we? Or being besieged in one for that matter.

There was a lot of shouting and ear deafening noise everywhere. But then it began to change and grow with the familiar sound of horses and knights hitting the ground as they finished clattering over the wooden drawbridge. The rapidly growing rain of arrows and the horses impaling their hoofs on the sharp points of the caltrops were doing their job.

It is what we expected and hoped.

Once one horse goes down in a narrow area those coming on fast behind it also begin going down as they crash into those who have gone down in front of them. That is particularly true in the darkness when the frantic horses and their riders cannot see well enough to avoid the downed horse and knights in front of them and do not have any place to go even if they do see them.

We could not see what was happening very well in the faint moonlight, but we could certainly hear it. Within seconds there were the sounds of what could only be a growing pile of screaming men and horses at the end of the drawbridge—and constant splashes as some the rearmost horses and riders were forced off the bridge and into the freezing water of the moat.

Behind the charging knights were their desperate men at arms and servants running hard in a desperate effort to escape. They added to the confusion and made things worse for the knights by trying to climb over the growing pile of kicking horses and struggling men in armour.

******

A few of the mounted men in the very front rank of the sortie succeeded in getting free and some of the French men at arms were able to climb over the huge and growing pile of horses and men and run away in the darkness. Most did not.

Hours later in the dawn's early light we began pulling the dead and injured men from the great mass of horses and men at the end of the drawbridge. It was obvious that many of the men and horses trapped at the bottom of the huge pile died of suffocation and being stepped on.

Later in the morning we began fishing drowned knights and men at arms out of moat to get their armour and weapons. But the water was so cold I quickly called off the effort—they will still be there in the summer.

Among the missing was Lady Alicia. She was not among the dead and injured. It was possible she was still in the castle so I sent a party of men under the command of one of our sergeants in through the tunnel. If they could get in without risking their lives they were to explore the castle whilst Thomas and I dealt with the prisoners.

The archers, men at arms, and the servants of the knights—the men stranded on the drawbridge and outside the castle gate because they followed the mounted knights, were taken prisoner. The castle's servants, however, were immediately freed—after they pointed out the knights and others among the survivors who had been with Henry FitzCount on the attack on Trematon or stood with him during his fraudulent challenge.

Most of the survivors had been at Trematon, the bastards, and now they were getting the fate they deserved—they were being tossed into the carts with the dead and wounded and taken shivering and moaning and crying for mercy to be thrown into the icy cold river.

******

What remained of Henry FitzCount disappeared whilst we were waiting to see who was still in the castle. Our men treated him like all the others. They stripped his body of his clothes and weapons and threw him and the bishop into one of the carts taking the similarly stripped dead and wounded knights and their soldiers for a swim in the Tamar to wash away their sins. It will be a permanent swim because their sins were so great for killing children and betraying their knightly oaths.

Besides, as I explained to Thomas, the ground is too frozen to dig and our men have worked hard enough. The knights' horses, of course, will be butchered and eaten unless they might still be usable. In which case they will be added to our small and growing herd of horses. Waste not, want not, as the good book says.

Thomas and I talked while we watched the casualties and prisoners being stripped, the carts being loaded with bodies and survivors destined for the river, and the knights' dead and injured horses cut up. We were waiting to approach the castle gate and our mood was dark as we watched the dead and wounded knights and their retainers being stripped of their armour and shoes and thrown into the carts.

The shrieks and pleas of the wounded knights and their men fell on deaf ears as they were thrown into the wagons and carried to the river—every one of our men had seen the butchered children and watched the dishonourable bastards ride away from the field outside of Trematon.

* * * * * *

Our victory at Launceton and the capture of the castle raised a number of questions that Thomas and I talked about to distract ourselves from the cold as we waited to enter the castle. Should we bring Sir Percy here to Launceston or move here ourselves or stay at Restormel?

What we decided as we stamped our feet and rubbed our arms was that we should stay at Restormel at least until next summer—primarily because that is where the boys were now in their school. Also because it is closer to the River Fowey where our galley and cogs were now anchored or pulled up on to the riverbank.

Whilst we waited and talked we also decided to name Martin the archer from London, one of the original archers, to be the commander at Launceston. Martin Archer was not the brightest candle in the lantern, but he was a steady fellow and we would leave Peter to be his second. Peter was the fast thinking sergeant who had the archers shooting at the sortieing knights even before Thomas and I got there to give the order. Sir Percy and his wife will stay at Trematon permanently as we had already promised them.

Whilst we stood there stamping our feet to stay warm we also talked about what we should do next and, in particular, whether our fleet of galleys should be based on the Tamar or on the Fowey over the winter. My initial thought was that the Tamar was too close to Devon and the Earl of Devon who was potentially unfriendly because he may or may not be one of FitzCount's cousins.

What I decided as we stood there in the cold was that we would stay at Restormel at least until spring arrived and buds and leaves suddenly spring out of the earth and dead branches to signal the start of a new year. Thomas nodded his agreement when I informed him.

What we also agreed as we stood there in the cold morning air and watched the sun rise was that the permanent location of our galleys and cogs was too important a question to answer quickly because the answer would affect where we ended up locating our permanent headquarters and training our new recruits.

Thomas and I were standing and talking just out of arrow range in front of the castle when the gate opened and the men who had entered through the tunnel waved us in. We searched everywhere but there was no sign of Alicia. She was not among the dead and wounded at the drawbridge and we did not find her in the castle.

The only people we found in the castle were its cowering servants and a handful of local men at who had wisely declined to join the escape effort. All will be pardoned and retained if they pledge their liege and were not present at Trematon.

And what if they had been present? Then they were sent to join the French knights and the bishop who were learning to swim in the Tamar.

Later that afternoon it finally dawned on me where Alicia might be. There must be another mine tunnel under the castle and Alicia who had come here to live with FitzCount was likely to know about it. I immediately sent a messenger asking Martin to question the servants and begin looking for other entrances to the mine under the castle.

Chapter Fifteen

Spring of 1193 arrived and leaves began springing out of the dead branches of the trees around Restormel. Unfortunately spring arrived at the same time the rivers began flooding throughout Cornwall when the rains come and the snows melted on the hills.

We responded by launching the beached galleys and floating everything down to the mouth of the Fowey. It was just as well—the time had come for me to take our galleys and cogs back to the Holy Land and earn more coins.

Getting coins while the getting is good is always the best policy. It is written in the Bible somewhere.

Thomas will be in charge whilst I am gone. He will stay at Restormel with George and the boys and a very strong force of men to discourage the Earl of Devon and his friends from attacking us.

Thomas's main task while I am gone will be to do what he truly loves to do—he will learn the boys to scribe and sum and, additionally, supervise the training and the assignments of any additional men we recruit from the steady stream of men who are constantly walking into our camp seeking to make their marks and join us.

He will also meet with the relatively few local franklins and the masters of Launceston's and the other manors to negotiate alternatives to their paying of their taxes and rents with coins—bringing us foodstuffs and firewood and horses, for example. *Horses for sure; we need more horses.*

Cornwall and my life was far more than I had ever dreamed would be possible. But, truth be told, I was getting bored and ready to head back to the Holy Land.

End of Book Two
Book three follows

The readers of these stories about what caused the dawn of Britain's age of greatness can be of good cheer about the possibility of more stories about the Great Wars that were about to engulf the archers. What will happen after that is uncertain. Oxford's taverns, however, are uncommonly good so there is every reason to hope that Martin Archer and his fellow scholars will continue the Oxford tradition of drinking and debating about what really happened in the medieval world until either someone with authority decides the story is complete, or they are forced out of their favourite pub by a shortage of Newcastle Ale.

There have been several close calls. For example, the scholars responsible for these pages almost stopped writing when Henry the Eighth had the heads chopped off several of them because they suggested that the company had prospered as a result of its relationship with the Pope. A memorial to them can be found in the Tom Quad of Christ Church College. Inquire at the porter's lodge just inside the tower gate.

There are more books in *The Company of Archers Saga*.

All of the books in this great saga of medieval England are available as individual eBooks, and some of them are also available in print and as audio books and multi-book collections. You can find them by searching for *Martin Archer stories*.

A bargain-priced collection of the entire first six books of the saga is available as *The Archers' Story*. Similarly, a collection of the next four books in the saga is available as *The Archers' Story: Part II;* the three novels after that as *The Archers' Story Part III;* and the four after that as *The Archers' Story: Part IV.*

A chronological list of all the books in the saga, and other books by Martin Archer, can be found below.

Finally, a word from Martin:

"I sincerely hope you enjoyed reading the latest story about my ancestors as much as I enjoyed writing it. If so, I respectfully request a favourable review on with as many stars as possible in order to encourage other readers.

"And, if you could please spare a moment, I would also very much appreciate your thoughts about this saga of medieval England, and whether you would like to see it continue. I can be reached at martinarcherV@gmail.com."

Cheers and thank you once again. /S/ Martin Archer

eBooks in the exciting and action-packed *The Company of Archers* saga:

The Archers

The Archers' Castle

The Archers' Return

The Archers' War

The Archers Stories IV – complete books XIV, XV, XVI, XVII

The Archers Stories V - complete books XVIII, XIX, XX

The Archers Stories VI - complete books XXI, XXII, XXIII

The Soldiers and Marines Saga - complete books I, II, III

Other eBooks you might enjoy:

Cage's Crew by Martin Archer writing as Raymond Casey

America's Next War by Michael Cameron – an adaption of Martin Archer's *War Breaks Out* to set it in the immediate future when Eastern and Western Europe go to war over another wave of Islamic refugees.

Sample pages from Book Three

The Archers Return

..... The big storm lasted almost two days. Then the weather cleared and we passed Gibraltar both rowing and running before the wind with our sails raised all the way up to the top of our two stubby masts.

We were not alone. One of our cogs, the one with the big patch on its forward sail captained by Albert the archer from Chester, came up on us fast due to the favourable wind. We had to row hard to keep up so we could talk as we passed the big rock with the huge Moorish castle on its peak.

But why are there no Moorish galleys here to collect tolls and taxes?

Harold and Albert managed to keep our two boats together until we reached the harbour at Palma two days later. To my absolute delight our other cog was already at anchor and so were four of our galleys.

There were happy hoys and waving arms from our friends as we entered the harbour and dropped the big rock that served as our anchor. Within minutes dinghies were rowing towards us from our other boats.

Palma is on Mallorca Island which is under the nominal control Moors called "Burburs" or something like that. What makes Mallorca a good place for us, and the reason we called in here for water and supplies, is that the Moors were in the midst a bloody civil war between their two main religious sects. As result, the island's Burbur ruler who chanted his prayers in one direction had become a deadly enemy of our Company's deadly enemies, the Moors of Tunis and Algiers who apparently chanted them in the other.

Moreover, as we knew from our last visit, Palma is apparently a fairly civilized place with many Christians and

Jews living on the island and a benign ruler. Both Genoa and Pisa have had shipping posts here for years.

We had returned to Palma once again for water and supplies because we did not have any problems when we rendezvoused here last year on our way to England. Also some of our galleys had successfully stopped here last fall on their way back to Cyprus from England.

Once again that seemed to be the case—the local Moors claimed to be pleased that we had given the Tunisians a poke in the eye. At least that was the story we got from the local merchants when we were last here.

"It is good to see everyone here and safe once again," I told the galley captains when they came aboard Harold's galley to report.

"Nothing's changed. We will leave here and rendezvous in Malta and then again in Cyprus as soon as the rest of our galleys arrive and the weather's good.

In the meantime you can all give your crews two hour shore leaves during daylight hours. But only a few men at a time and no one is to go ashore after dark.

Explain to your men why they have to stay close—it is because we want to be always ready to fight in case Moorish pirates come into the harbour looking for a fight and also because we will be leaving for Malta as soon as the rest of our boats arrive and finish taking on supplies."

We want everyone to think we are going to Malta from here. We are not.

End of Sample Page

Made in the USA
Las Vegas, NV
24 September 2023

78097398R00121